FIRST KILL

An Eli Quinn Mystery

Robert Roy Britt

Published by Ink • Spot Books
P.O. Box 74693
Phoenix, Arizona 85087
InkSpotBooks.com
Published in the United States of America
First printing, 2016

Cover by Trent Design

First Kill/Robert Roy Britt. 1st ed.
ISBN 978-0-9977614-2-9

DRONE

"A brisk detective novel sequel that packs a punch."
— *Kirkus Reviews*

"Quinn's second case reads as if it were written by a master reaching the height of his craft. With its witty banter, cast of colorful secondary characters, and promising detective agency, DRONE sidles into the genre with aplomb. ... Characterizations are top notch, the plot is believably paced with ratcheting tension, and the prose is highly polished. ... Quinn's personality gives him an everyman feel that makes him easy to connect with. Unlike more intellectual literary detectives, Quinn is relatable and fun to root for."

★★★★★
— *Foreword Clarion Reviews*

"Fast-paced with a few thought-provoking twists, DRONE is reminiscent of a noir detective story with a 21st century flair." ★★★★★
— *IndieReader*

"Immediately absorbing and thoroughly entertaining."
— *Bestsellerworld.com*

"Robert Roy Britt's writing is engaging and captivating – written both with a mature slant and just a little camp. Britt takes on a well-trod genre and introduces a distinct yet fitting addition to its hall of fame. Both brilliant and humble, hard-nosed and gentle, Eli Quinn's mettle is thoroughly tested in curious and entertaining ways. It's hard to make an original detective, but Britt is more than up to the challenge. He does a wonderful job of telling this twisting tale with excellent pace."
— *Self-Publishing Review*

For Nourie, Yacine & Marius, the lights of my life

CHAPTER 1

The tall man drove into the circular entrance of the hotel, parked away from the valets. The real estate agent would find him, would choose to look at property rather than stay at the convention. Realtors would die to get a listing like this, acreage that would fetch a premium.

He didn't care about any of that. His role was simple.

The agent came out, walked over. Expensive casual business clothes hung perfectly on a stocky frame. He introduced himself and got in.

On the way to the property, they made polite conversation about the Arizona heat and the growing humidity. The tall man tugged down on his black baseball cap, pulling it low over his eyes. He answered the agent's questions without any extra chit-chat. Was in the Marines. Grenade. Helping his dad sell this old ranch house. Ten acres. Great views.

The real estate agent wouldn't shut up. Typical salesman. On and on about his company, about his whip-smart daughter, who would one day take over the business. His gorgeous wife was a handful. But they'd been together since high school, and she could sell houses like nobody's business, and for some crazy reason he still loved her.

The tall man nodded, tugged on his cap. It'd be a pleasure to kill this guy.

The last half-mile was bumpy and dusty, older homes each on several acres. Thirsty mesquite trees hugged the landscape. Saguaros stood sentry at irregular intervals, arms up, praying for rain.

He drove down into a dry arroyo, slowed for the curb-height drop into the sandy bottom, then gunned it to avoid getting stuck. He eased up as they pulled out onto a broad, isolated mesa. The stocky man blathered on about how the road could be improved. The tall one just listened. They pulled up to the ramshackle home. The vast, sparse desert ran off into distant mountains. Some wealthy East Coaster would pay handsomely for the land, knock the home down and build a sprawling territorial house. But his father didn't want to sell. And then this opportunity arose. He had little choice.

They got out, a cloud of dust catching up and drifting by. He gestured to the front entrance and followed the agent into the shadows of a crudely constructed porch. Then with one powerful blow, the side of his fist connected with the man's temple and he crumpled to the ground.

CHAPTER 2

Madison Mack stabbed her finger in Jimmy Mendoza's chest, her nose to his chin as they stood on the sidewalk. I pulled up to the curb across the street in my Jeep, top down. Solo watched them from the back seat, ears up, nose twitching.

"Stay," I said to the 110-pound German shepherd. I knew he would, as long as the situation called for it. I hopped out and walked into the argument.

I'd never met Madison Mack but she was easy to recognize. Her father Joe ran the biggest real estate agency in Pleasant, just north of Scottsdale in the shadow of Pinnacle Peak. Joe's wife Joanne and Madison both worked for him. Madison's face was plastered all over town, in newspaper ads, flyers, on the Open House sign behind her in the front yard, and on the side of the dark metallic blue Tesla in the driveway.

Fifteen minutes ago she'd called and asked me to meet her at this home she was showing, said she had a case for me but she'd be stuck at an open house most of the day. I'd been wading through a stack of bills at my new office, including the outrageous electric bill, while wondering where my next case would come from. I locked the office, crossed the small town and arrived five minutes early.

Their conversation wasn't meant for me, but my hearing is excellent, and I caught most of it as I crossed the street.

"Jimmy, don't tell me you haven't seen or heard from him," Madison said. She had one hand on a small purse strapped over her shoulder, a thumb in the purse, ready to reach into it if needed. "You were with him at the conference."

"Hell, Madison, c'mon," said Jimmy Mendoza, hint of an accent sneaking out with his frustration. "I saw him in the morning. Then I didn't see him after that. That's all I know."

I'd also never met Jimmy Mendoza, another real estate agent whose photo you couldn't escape, including on the door of his black Lexus at the curb. Easy for them to remember which car was whose.

She lowered her voice. "You screw with me, Jimmy, I'll ruin you." She poked again to punctuate the threat. "I know about the…" She stopped as I approached.

Jimmy grabbed her by the wrist. "Don't threaten me, Madison. It goes both ways. You know that." She glared at him, started reaching into her purse.

That's when I tapped Jimmy on the shoulder. He turned his head, held her wrist.

"Who the hell are you?"

"Eli Quinn," I said. I nodded my head toward his grip. "Let go."

Jimmy was neat and tidy, in a perfectly fitting casual suit, no tie. Short black hair on top, shaved on the sides. He had the look of a fighter in his eye, someone who chose to stand his ground, not back down. I knew how to fight, too. Maybe he knew that, maybe he didn't. But he let go of Madison, took a step back and raised his hands like a criminal. That's when I heard Solo growl. He stood next to me, giving Jimmy Mendoza his most threatening glare, which

4

resembles his other looks but without his tongue lolling to the side.

"Look, man." Jimmy talked to me but eyed Solo. "This is between me and Madison, okay? Everything's cool. Anyway, it's none of your business."

"You made it my business when you grabbed her," I said.

"I can take care of myself," Madison said, still watching Jimmy.

I raised my eyebrows at Madison, then looked at Jimmy to see what his next move would be. And I wondered why the hell I was here.

Jimmy glanced my way, narrowed his gaze, then his eyes hopped over to Madison and he shook his head. "To hell with this," he said, pointing at Madison as he headed to his car. "This is *not* over."

***

Madison Mack defied the early morning Arizona heat and humidity in a black, tailored suit with a skirt cut just above the knee. She was a mid-twenties twin of her mid-forties mother, except Madison hadn't bleached her dark brown hair, and she wore it long, and she had barely a touch of makeup on. And she didn't have her mother's fake boobs. Madison was the more attractive of the two, but since she was about ten years younger than me, and since I was head over heels for someone else, I tried hard not to pay attention to Madison's good looks. The effort failed miserably.

"Mr. Quinn."

"Just Quinn."

"Madison Mack." She stuck her hand out business-like. We shook. The hand was thin but the handshake firm.

"Good-looking dog," she said, nodding at Solo. He wagged his tail. "Scared the hell out of Jimmy Mendoza."

"You sure that wasn't me did the scaring?"

She rolled her eyes. "I'm sure. Jimmy's a hothead, quick to get into it. I don't think you'd scare him. And like I said, you didn't need to rush in on your white horse."

"Gun in the purse?" I pointed at it.

"Like I said, I can take care of myself. But I also know when to hire someone. Can I hire you?"

"That depends."

"On what?"

"On why."

"My dad is missing." Her business face clouded over.

"Joe Mack is missing?"

"Since about noon yesterday."

"Sorry, didn't know." I pointed at my battered face. "Been a little out of it."

"You do look like hell," she said.

I laughed. It hurt. I stopped laughing.

"What's funny?"

"Nothing," I said. "Just that I've heard that quite a bit lately."

My lip was still puffy, six stitches due to come out later today. My swollen eye had opened up, but the white part was red. The bruise on my cheek had turned from blue to vomit yellow. And my ribs still hurt.

Two cases into this private detective thing and I was a mess. A few bad guys were even worse off. With help from a small, informal team I was developing, I'd just nabbed the guy who tried to assassinate a state senator and uncovered the even worse act he was engaged in. Before that, I'd solved the Tinker Bernstein murder. I hoped my next case would involve fewer injuries.

"I saw on TV," she said. "They called you a hero."

"I'd reserve that word for people who do far greater things."

"They said you're a genius detective."

That was hard to argue with, so I shrugged.

"Let's get out of the heat," she said, nodding at the house. I followed her to the front door. She fitted a key into the lock. "No dogs."

"No dogs, no Quinn," I said, having learned on my last case to keep Solo as close as possible at all times.

She glanced at Solo, then pushed the door open. "He won't crap on the carpet?"

"Not unless I ask him to."

The house was empty and spotless. Mack Realty brochures sat on the kitchen counter, a picture of Madison on the cover. I picked one up and turned it over. A photo of Joe Mack was on the back. I stuck the brochure in my back pocket, told Solo to lie down in the kitchen. He curled up with gusto, always excited to do nothing. Madison walked through the living room to a wall of windows, stood looking out at the small backyard and the nice view of Pinnacle Peak, hands clasped behind her back.

"Can you find my father?"

"I don't know yet. Tell me what happened."

Her voice was even, her back to me. "He went to a real estate conference at the Princess hotel in Scottsdale yesterday. All-day thing. I called him in the afternoon and he didn't answer. I texted him, no reply. He always replies to my texts. I tried a couple hours later and still nothing. Nobody has seen him since."

"Did you call the Scottsdale police?"

She turned and glared at me. "Of course. Do you think I'm an idiot?"

I didn't have much to go on, but her eyes, green and complex as a stormy sea, suggested she was not an idiot. "No, Ms. Mack. You seem very capable."

"Madison," she said.

I nodded. "Ms. Mack, it's been less than twenty-four hours. You sure he's missing?"

"The police asked me the same thing. But yes, I'm sure. He would have returned my texts, at least. They said they'd

7

look into it, but they didn't seem to be in a rush."

"Maybe his phone died."

"He'd have found a way to call the office and check in. He's compulsive that way. I don't remember a morning when he didn't check in."

"Did you call the hotel?"

"Of course," she said. "They don't know anything. He didn't have a room, so they have no record of him being there."

"Has he ever disappeared before, maybe overnight or something?"

"Of course not. Nobody is more responsible than my father." A quick tug at her light summer blazer closed that matter.

"What were you arguing with Jimmy Mendoza about?" I pointed with my thumb to the front of the house.

She looked away, then turned and went back to the windows. "We were fighting over the listing of this house. He thought he'd get it. I got it."

"Strike one," I said.

She turned. "Excuse me?"

"That's your first lie."

Her face flushed.

"You accused Jimmy of knowing where your father was," I said.

"You have excellent hearing."

"And we're off to a bad start," I said. "I can't work for someone who's going to lie to me."

"I'm sorry." She closed her eyes and cupped her forehead, let out a sigh, then put herself back together quickly. "It won't happen again."

"What'd you threaten him about? Something about knowing something else."

"Jimmy and Dad go way back," Madison said.

"Bad blood?"

"Jimmy's the third biggest agent in town. They respect

each other, and they get along well enough, but no question Jimmy is jealous of Dad. They've had arguments, and Jimmy threatened Dad with lawsuits a couple times, but they always managed to work things out."

"Sounds like a suspect."

"See, you *are* a genius detective." She smiled and, for the first time, looked like her photo, but prettier. Lively face, strong cheekbones, slight overbite.

I found the business-like nature of our conversation curious, like a boardroom meeting or a conversation I might've had in the newsroom at *The Arizona Republic*, back when I was a reporter. But everyone dealt with stress differently. I weighed all this. She watched me weigh it. Then she walked toward me, stopped a few feet away, put one hand on a hip and smoothed her hair with the other. Her voice was strong and her face stern.

"Listen. I love my dad. And for now I assume he's alive and everything's OK. I can't believe otherwise. He'd want me to be strong, keep my emotions in check and take care of business."

"What about your mother?"

Madison folded her arms. Her eyes became slits and the words spilled out. "She's a total…" She caught herself, the professional Madison wrestling with the personal. Blinked. "Let's call her high maintenance."

"Aha."

"What?"

"I don't know," I said. "Maybe your dad couldn't take her anymore, ran off with someone else."

"Fuck you, Quinn."

No smart retorts came to mind, so I waited. She waited. I was no expert in detective-client relations yet, but I was pretty sure things weren't off to a great start with my third prospective client. When the waiting became a staring match, I asked the obvious question any genius detective would ask.

"Your dad have other enemies besides Jimmy Mendoza?"

Madison turned around, walked to a door that opened onto the back patio. "There are too many to count. Real estate business in Pleasant is competitive as hell. Dad runs the top agency in town, so we're a target for lots of name-calling, false rumors, petty crap like that."

She opened the door, went out into the backyard. Solo got up and we followed her out.

They say it's a dry heat, and that's true when it is dry. It's not true when the monsoon moisture moves in. I don't sweat easily, but five minutes in this weather and I would.

"Other agents have it in for your dad?"

She walked around a small oval putting green, artificial turf with a cup and flag, and followed a tidy flagstone path to the back fence. Pinnacle Peak anchored the view, its jumble of orange-red rock jutting into the blue sky, thunderheads already building behind it. She faced the view, hands clasped behind her back again.

"I don't know. Maybe. Probably. Sure."

"Names?"

"Nobody else I can pinpoint. Dad runs the business. I mostly just sell houses. He's taught me a lot about the real estate business, but day-to-day I stay out of the schmoozing and the politics and all the bickering."

"Why not let the police handle this?"

She raised her voice, flung a hand up in frustration, flicking her fingers into the air. "That's what *Mother* said."

"Not bad advice."

"Mother rarely gives good advice. And Mack Realty doesn't exist without Dad. If I don't find him, my mother takes over the business. She's manipulative, controlling."

"In what way?"

"This is all in confidence."

"Of course," I said.

"She has a weakness for plastic surgery. She uses her, uh,

assets to get listings and sell houses. When a place needs work, she can get a contractor or a pool boy to do just about anything, always at a discount. But she knows nothing about accounting, advertising, managing a team, running the business. I could do it all, but she wouldn't let me. We barely speak."

"So you love your dad," I said.

She turned and faced me from across the fake lawn. "And I need him." Her face softened the tiniest bit. "Will you help me?"

I squinted and gave her my best detective-in-thinking-mode look, useful when I don't know what to say. My first case had come easy, suggested by the amazing and utterly delightful Samantha Marcos as a way to get my life going again a year after I'd lost my wife. My second case fell from the sky. Now here was my potential third client, and the case sounded like a mess waiting to be stepped in. I decided to remain undecided. And so I shrugged.

"You're not sure," she said.

"I'm not sure the case is a good fit."

"What do you normally charge?"

"So far, a dollar."

She laughed, sharp, brief, dismissive.

"I try to do good things," I said. "Help people." I didn't tell her about the investments from my Wall Street days. Or that they'd stagnated in my years as a reporter, then dwindled when I left the paper and spent a year chasing my wife's killer. Or that my new office came with a steep monthly rent, and the first electric bill had shocked me and summer was just getting started.

"A real estate agent doesn't work as hard when the commission is four percent as when it's six percent," she said. "I expect you to work your ass off on this, so please quote me the going rate."

I pondered that. Some cash flow would be useful to pay bills. But I'd resolved not to take cases just to make money.

There was plenty not to like about this one, but my gut told me Madison Mack was genuine, and genuinely in need. I looked over at Solo. He didn't seem to object. I cited a reasonable daily rate.

"And you'll focus on this exclusively?"

"I have nothing else pressing." I had nothing else, period.

"Done," she said.

"Plus expenses." I was getting the hang of this.

"Like what?"

"No clue."

"Fine." She waved me away. "Go find my Dad now. I have a house to sell."

CHAPTER 3

My new office was perfectly situated a block north of Lulu's Grind, the greatest coffee shop in Pleasant, probably in all of Arizona, possibly in the world. Solo and I locked the office and walked south on Pleasant Way, crossed Easy Street and found Samantha Marcos holding a table for two on Lulu's patio.

The late morning heat pushed most people inside, but shade made the patio bearable. Clouds billowed overhead, blocked the sun. Sam stood as we walked up.

I thought Sam might kiss me. We were, after all, a thing now. We'd held hands for the first time just the other day. Looked into each others' eyes finally knowing that what had been building for a year had taken its natural course to the inevitable. But there hadn't been time yet to take the relationship beyond the initial, glorious realization, to establish any customs. And given our long history together, and being in our mid-thirties, and me having lost my wife just over a year ago, it was unclear how quickly we'd move through the various phases of courtship, if that was even still a thing.

Before we sat down Solo got a kiss, returned it with a

major face-lick, and then Sam scratched him behind the ears. It wasn't clear who Sam loved most, me or my German shepherd. I took the opportunity to admire Sam, in her tan shorts, a sleeveless white tee that made her olive skin darker, simple brown leather sandals. It was about as much attire as Sam ever wore. It was all she needed.

After Solo was satisfied, he sat and let me have a turn. Sam wrapped her arms around me and leaned her head against my chest. My insides turned mushy.

"Ribs," I reminded her.

"I know," she said, and she didn't squeeze. She pulled back and looked up at me. "And hey, you owe me a first kiss."

I pointed at my fat lip.

"Yeah," she said, "we'll wait until it doesn't look like a pregnant banana slug."

"It's healing."

"Make it quick," she said.

She kissed my cheek—the one that wasn't vomit yellow—and brushed her fingers across my fat lip. I curled a strand of her long black hair behind her ear, the way I'd seen her do many times. Then we stood there a moment, like teenagers, looking at each other. One could stare at Sam Marcos for hours. Of course I never did during our long friendship. But now, I had a license to get totally lost in those deep brown eyes.

Lulu walked up. Solo stuck his nose in and pried me and Sam apart.

"Finally," Lulu said in her sing-song Tanzanian accent. "I tell you, right? Eli Quinn, go have sex. Have a life."

Lulu was tall and thin, dark and sexy. And sassy.

"No sex yet," Sam said.

"His face?" Lulu gestured at my present hideousness, made a face of her own.

"That, too," Sam said. "Plus this is, technically, our first date."

14

"Pish-posh," Lulu said, waving a graceful hand in the air.

"Hello?" I said. "I'm standing right here?"

They laughed and air kissed. I sat. Sam sat. Solo sat next to Sam.

"Is hot out for coffee," Lulu said. "Everybody else inside."

"Never too hot for your coffee," I said.

"Make it two," Sam said.

We both knew not to order lattes or any other coffee perversions. Lulu didn't make them. Yet the place was packed every morning.

"Coffee come right up." Lulu headed inside, turning around once to flash me one of her winning, mischievous grins.

"Lulu is a fan of yours," Sam said.

"She was Jess' best friend."

Sam nodded.

This wasn't an easy discussion, but it was necessary. "You know that, right?"

Sam nodded. Sam didn't nod much. That was my thing. Sam usually just said what was on her mind.

"And now she's becoming a friend of yours," I said.

Another nod. She blinked and curled her straight black hair behind an ear.

"I'm OK with that," I said.

"I know, Quinn. I'll be fine with all this." She spread her arms to encompass the whole town and our new relationship. "But your past will always be with us, and sometimes I won't know exactly what to do with it."

"You're not jealous."

"Not of Lulu. Should I be?"

"No," I said. "Of Jess, though?"

Sam had been a good friend when we worked together at the newspaper. She became a great friend throughout my year of chasing down Jess' killer, had been instrumental in helping me find him. Now we were starting another phase.

It had been a long, gradual process, a natural one that had to go slow until it felt right. I reached out and put my hand on hers.

"Not really jealous," she said. "Just, maybe ... a little awkward."

"Awkward has never really been a problem for you and me."

"I'm human."

"But you'll be OK with all this, with us."

"Will you?"

I nodded.

"Then so will I," she said.

"And we'll still have that first kiss."

"Without question," she said.

"And it'll be good."

"You have no idea."

Lulu brought two coffees and set them down, smiled again. We thanked her and she went back inside.

"So," Sam said. "How was your first day back at the office?"

"Someone called me a genius detective."

Sam laughed, a brief outburst so delightful I wished it would just last and last.

"She hired me."

"Congratulations!" She smiled wide and punched my shoulder, a little harder than necessary. Solo wagged his tail. Seriously, attack dog? "Your third case."

"Madison Mack," I said.

"Oh," Sam said. "Now I *am* jealous."

"No need. She's too young."

"Hot, though."

"Definitely hot," I said. "And loaded."

"She wants you to find her dad."

"You know about Joe Mack."

"Everybody knows."

"Except me."

16

"You were convalescing."

"And drinking," I said.

"Part of convalescing."

Sam sipped her coffee, kept her eyes on me. I'd never thought of coffee drinking as sexy before. I told her about the case.

"You know what happened?"

"Nope," I said.

"Any theories?"

"Nope."

"Clues? Leads?"

"Nope."

"For a detective, it seems there's a lot you don't know."

I shrugged. "Been on the case an hour. Something will turn up."

"What's your first step?"

"Go talk with Aahna Chaudhari."

"Your landlord."

"And the Number Two real estate agent in town. She knows everybody."

"She totally has the hots for you," Sam said.

"Jealous?"

"Should I be?"

"Nope," I said. "Aahna's not my type."

"What's your type?"

"You."

"Good answer."

CHAPTER 4

Aahna Chaudhari's outer office oozed rich, warm colors that made you feel like you were in a tropical sunset. Water trickled down a vertical, floor-to-ceiling slate fountain along one wall. Her young secretary had purple hair in a ponytail, fair skin well-tanned. A gold nameplate said Becca Jones. She winced when she saw the swelling and bruises on my face then told me to please take a seat, Aahna was busy and she didn't know if I'd be able to see her now.

Aahna spotted me through the inner window to her office and waved me in. The secretary threw up her hands. Aahna clicked off her cell phone as I walked in.

"Eli Quinn." She stated it like a discovery, in her deep, rich voice, then sat on the corner of her desk, looked me up and down. My jeans, gray tee and running shoes were no match for her sharp gray suit that barely held her curves in place while screaming real estate. Long, black curly hair went in all directions. Dark eyebrows arched over large eyes.

"You look like hell," she said. Aahna spoke at her own pace, drawing her words out. She never seemed to be in a rush.

"So I've heard."

"I'd still do you in a heartbeat."

"If only I were available." It was a game we played. Well, for me it was just a game.

She raised one of her excellent eyebrows. "That Samantha woman?"

"Yep."

"I knew it," she said. She spun around and sat in her chair, steepled her fingers, and stared at me across the desk. "Too bad, Quinn. Hearts will be broken."

I shrugged.

"So you didn't come to seduce me. What can I do for you?"

I gestured to her client chair. "May I?"

"Please."

I closed her office door and sat down. "Madison Mack hired me to find her dad. You heard he's missing."

"I did hear. Since yesterday. I hope everything's OK. Maybe he just needed to get away from his wife. God knows she's a b-i-t-c-h."

The verdict on Joanne Mack seemed unanimous.

"Tell me about Joanne."

"She's a powerful woman in this town. She gets what she wants."

"No crime in that."

"She has methods that, shall we say, go beyond business practices I'm willing to undertake."

"She uses all her assets," I said.

"Business practices I'm not willing to gossip about."

"And you know this how?"

"It's not really a secret, so I suppose this isn't gossiping. She pushes everyone around. She's got money, connections, and those other assets. But if she wasn't married to Joe Mack, honestly, she'd be nothing. I don't know how she puts up with her."

"What do you think of Madison?"

"Good kid. Too serious or, I don't know…"

"Severe?"

"Exactly," she said. "Really good at what she does. Treats people fairly. Smart agent. I'd hire her if I could."

I pondered all that. It didn't mean much. Yet. Aahna watched me think, then she asked, "So what's going on?"

"Madison doesn't think her dad would just run off, not call her, not call the office."

"Neither do I. It doesn't sound like Joe."

"I was hoping you could help me figure out what other possibilities there are," I said.

"Like what?"

"Joe Mack annoy anyone?"

Aahna laughed with her whole body, a brief loud cackle then rolling chuckles as she composed herself, knuckle to a nostril like a cork. "Just about every agent in town."

"Tell me about that."

"Joe's really good at what he does. And he's wealthy. He's got so many people working for him that he doesn't have to get his hands dirty anymore."

"Realtors get their hands dirty?"

"Metaphorically. Endless hours chasing down listings, showing a house a gazillion times to make a sale, mountains of paperwork. Early mornings, late nights. Weekends. Holidays."

"So what's he do?"

"He golfs, schmoozes, meets and greets. Consummate networker. And he spends a fortune on advertising. Nobody is more aggressive than Mack Realty. The listings just flow in. Joe doles them out to his best agents, keeping the very best listings in the family."

"Madison and Joanne."

"Exactly. He takes a cut of every commission. He almost never sells a house himself. It's a gold mine."

"Nothing breeds enemies like success," I said.

"Exactly. So you think someone's done something to

20

Joe?"

Other than the suspicions of Madison, all I had were hunches. The Scottsdale Police told me they had no leads. Even if they did, they probably wouldn't tell some upstart private eye who they didn't know. The sheriff's department just hung up on me. I'd made the quick drive down to the Fairmont Scottsdale Princess, interviewed the hotel manager, who repeated what he'd told the police: Nobody saw anything unusual. I spoke to the conference organizer, who said she wouldn't notice one person out of five-hundred attendees leaving the conference early. I didn't burden Aahna with any of this.

"Don't know," I said. "Have to consider it. And it sounds like the list of suspects is, what, every real estate agent in town?"

"You could start there," she said.

"You hate him?"

"Me? No. I'm OK with success. He's earned what he has. He plays by the rules and treats people well."

"Plus you're doing pretty well yourself. Number Two agent in Pleasant."

"I am." She smiled and leaned back in her chair.

"That annoy some people?"

"Not as much as Joe Mack annoys them, but yes."

"Anybody try to kill you?"

"Not yet."

"You kill Joe?"

"If I did I wouldn't tell you." She arched an eyebrow and smiled like the devil.

"What else can you tell me about the Macks?"

Aahna blinked, smile fading. She licked her lips and looked through the window where the secretary tapped away at a keyboard. "Probably not relevant."

"But you're going to tell me anyway."

"If it helps find Joe. But you'll be discreet with this?"

"As discreet as I can be," I said.

She took a deep breath, sighed.

"OK. You didn't get this from me. I'm not a gossip, and I can't afford to get a reputation for being one. And I don't even know how much of this is true."

"I already can't remember where I heard this."

Aahna nodded slowly, three times. "Rumor is Joe and Joanne are swingers."

"I see. And you don't mean fashionable and trendy."

"I mean sleeping with other couples."

The mess I worried about stepping in just got messier. "Any idea who they swing with?"

"You thinking of a lifestyle change, Quinn?"

"Nope. I've got Sam Marcos, remember?"

"I *keeel* her."

"Jeff Dunham," I said. "Achmed."

"Very good."

"Anyway," I said, "No. Not planning to swing. But maybe I'll need to go check them out, at least."

"Should be fun," she said. She tapped her desk with the fingers of both hands, stalling. Finally she said, "Some people talk more than they should." She nodded toward the reception room where Becca Jones was filing things.

I looked over my shoulder at the young woman in the purple ponytail. "And what's she talk about?"

"Nothing I've heard that would help you. I just get the drift of things from one side of her phone conversations."

"So she talks to swingers on the phone at work."

"Millennials have a different sense of the workplace than our generation."

"You think they use email, too?"

"Maybe," Aahna said.

"You think she'd be dumb enough to use her work email for this?"

Aahna sighed, shrugged.

"And you, being the owner of this place, you could access her email."

"You mean hack it."

"Technically it wouldn't be hacking. You're within your rights to monitor her work email."

"She's a good kid. I'd hate to get her in trouble. And anyway, there's no law against swinging."

"If I promise to keep her out of it?"

"I don't know."

"For Joe's sake? For Madison?"

Aahna sat forward, put her elbows on her desk, hands together in a prayer-like gesture, fingers pressed against her lips. She stared at me a moment, then nodded.

"Call me?"

She nodded, and I left.

CHAPTER 5

Solo snored in the corner of my office, curled up on his dog bed. The air conditioner in the front window fought mightily against the heat and humidity. I made coffee, poured a cup, and sat behind my old oak desk in the world's most comfortable chair, put my running shoes up on the desk, and spent the rest of the afternoon mulling the case.

There was almost nothing to go on. I had one suspect in Jimmy Mendoza. I ran a background check on him—it's remarkable what you can find about a person via the internet—and didn't turn up anything to suggest he was a murderer or a kidnapper. There were dozens of other potential suspects among the many real estate agents in Pleasant who might have a grudge against Joe Mack. And for all I knew, Joe had simply skipped town.

Meanwhile, my client had lied to me before she was even my client. Madison was an arm-folder, one of those people who always seems to be on guard. Who knows what else she might be hiding. And now the swinging lifestyle had been thrown into the mix. I considered the likelihood that Madison knew her parents were swingers. That'd be another lie, or at least an interesting omission.

"Why the hell did I take this case?"

Solo stopped snoring long enough to open one eye and sneeze, shaking his head, then he went back to sleep. Solo was really good at finding and attacking bad guys. And sleeping. Not much of a conversationalist.

I knew why I'd taken the case, though. Despite her tough exterior, Madison Mack was genuinely worried about her father. I knew what it was like to lose someone important. Plus, from everything I knew, Joe Mack was a good guy, an upstanding businessman, a father whose daughter loved him. I looked over the stack of bills on the edge of my desk. The reasons to take the case outweighed the reasons not to.

***

I answered my iPhone on the first ring. "Hey, Aahna."

"I feel dirty, Quinn."

"You got into her email."

"First I'm a gossip. Now I'm a hacker. Remind me why I'm helping you?"

"Because you love the Macks?"

Aahna forced a cough.

"Because you're a good person, and this is the right thing to do?"

"Eh."

"Because I'm a hunk?"

"Now you're talking."

"What'd you learn?"

"Nothing."

"Nothing?"

"Becca doesn't use her work email for anything inappropriate."

That was no surprise. Email was to a millennial what the written letter was to a baby boomer. "She text a lot?"

"Constantly," Aahna said.

I thought about that. The outlines of an idea formed quickly.

"Quinn?"

"I'm here," I said. Then I told her what I had in mind.

"I don't know…"

"Aahna. You don't want to drag Becca into this mess. I understand. But from where I sit, it looks like she might be in the middle of it already. I could just go talk to her, but then she'd be involved for sure, and she might do something stupid, I don't know, even put herself in danger. I need to know what's going on, and if she hasn't done anything wrong, then I'll keep her out of it."

"And your plan will do all that."

"Might."

She hesitated just a moment. "When?"

"I'll be there in ten minutes." I hung up and called Sam, explained the scheme to her. Then I woke Solo up and we headed out to the Jeep.

*****

I drove back to Aahna Chaudhari's office, left Solo in the Jeep with the top down in the shade, and walked back into the office with the perpetual sunset.

"Me again," I said to Becca. "To see Aahna again."

"She's not here."

"That's OK. I'll wait."

"She might be awhile. You can have a seat if you like." She gestured to the guest chairs.

"Thank you," I said, polite as could be. I took a seat and, without letting her see my phone, sent the prewritten group text to Sam and Aahna to let them know I was ready, then I slipped the phone into my back pocket.

Becca's cell phone rang. She answered, said hello, and frowned.

"It's for you," she said. "Someone named Samantha. She

said it's an emergency and you're not answering your phone."

I reached to the holster on my hip. "Ah, crap. I left it at the office. How'd Sam get your number?"

"She called Aahna." Becca handed me her phone. "Here."

"Hey Sam, what's up?"

"You're welcome," Sam said. "Good luck." And she hung up.

I uttered some words of concern. "Yeah … Uh-huh … You're sure? … Oh, no." I was running out of words when Aahna came through the door, the day's heat billowing in around her.

"Quinn," she said.

I held up a finger to show I was busy. "Uh-huh … OK … Sure I can."

Aahna spoke to Becca: "C'mere, I need to show you something." She led Becca into her office to look at who knows what.

While Becca was in Aahna's office, her back to me, I flipped through her text messages. There were several just from today. I scrolled down, found one that started "It'll be fun" and opened the thread, an exchange with someone named Donovan Fisk. Didn't take long to get the gist. "Just a toga … they r open-minded … u will love the lifestyle … tonite at 9."

I scrolled back further and found a text from Jimmy Mendoza. "U, donovan if he's game, me n rachael, bo n his wife."

I closed the messaging app and opened the phone app, then hit the off button, walked into Aahna's office and gave Becca her phone. "Thank you," I said. "Emergency resolved. All is well."

Aahna handed Becca a folder. "The list is in here," she said. "Go ahead and start now." Becca took the folder, with whatever made-up work was in it, excused herself around me and went back to her desk.

I closed the door and sat in the client chair facing Aahna. She was paler than usual.

"It's a dirty job," I said.

"It's your dirty job." She curled a lip in disgust. "Don't ask me to do that again."

"I won't," I said. "And thank you."

She nodded. "What'd you find?"

"I'm going to try and go swinging tonight."

"Who with?"

"You won't believe it," I said.

"I'll believe just about anything at this point."

"Jimmy Mendoza and his wife."

"Rachael." Aahna smirked, but didn't look too surprised. The color was back in her face.

"I thought Jimmy and Joe Mack don't get along."

"They've had their disagreements," Aahna said. "Jimmy's a loudmouth, real hothead."

"I've seen."

"Just about every agent in town has been on the receiving end of one of his tirades at some point. He actually punched one of my agents once."

"Real estate's a tough business, I hear."

"Jimmy had an offer on a house, my agent swooped in with a cash offer from a Canadian buyer. It was two grand less than Jimmy's offer, but the buyer took the cash. Jimmy was so mad, he just lost it."

"How did it end?"

"Nothing broken. Jimmy apologized. He's not a bad guy. Just can't control his temper. Anyway, Jimmy and Joe both have good-looking wives, and I suppose men will see past business for one thing."

"I've heard."

"Anyone else?" Aahna sounded interested now. I might've kept the names to myself, but I trusted her, and she was giving me good insights in return.

"Someone named Bo," I said. "I assume that's Bo Rollins, the former Mets pitcher."

"Probably a good guess. Bo works for Park Realtors. I've seen him hanging out socially with Jimmy before. Bo sells a few houses, but he's a minor leaguer in real estate. Moves maybe one a month."

"I used to live in New York," I said. "Wasn't exactly a fan of Rollins, but…"

"Don't tell me you're a Mets fan."

"Guilty."

"Poor thing," she said.

"What's he like?"

"He's cocky. You know, a former ballplayer, tall and good-looking. He thinks the world owes him something."

"Hell, his lifetime ERA was 4.52," I said. "He owes Mets fans something."

"I don't know much about that. But he's got a sexy wife, too. Bleach-blonde hair, gym body, fake, um, assets, like the others. Hasn't worked a day in her life."

"So these three real estate agents have their wives on the market, as it were."

"I don't know how it works," Aahna said. "But from the rumors I've heard, the men are on the market, too."

"And someone named Donovan Fisk. He's your secretary's current squeeze, it seems."

"Don't recognize the name. Becca's love life is a revolving door. And apparently swingers are always seeking new recruits. Rumor is they leave the garage door partway open as a signal. Other swingers cruise around Pleasant looking for the signal."

"Lotta rumors," I said.

"Lotta crazy stuff."

I nodded at that. "Thanks, Aahna," I said. "You've helped."

"I hope you'll return the favor someday."

"If it weren't for Sam Marcos, I'd certainly consider it."

CHAPTER 6

As darkness fell the next day, the tall man went out to the shed, unlocked it, snipped the zip ties from the real estate agent's ankles, and yanked him to his feet. He left the man's wrists tied, mouth duct taped. The agent would be hungry and dehydrated, more than a day in the shed. No energy, no resistance. Quiet. Unseen. Easy.

He would've done this last night, but he had to wait for an opportunity when he wouldn't be seen. Now it was time, and it would be over quickly. He was looking forward to it.

The man twisted fruitlessly, tried to kick his captor and stumbled as he was pushed out of the shed, then around the side of the house, and down a trail out back.

Failed thunderclouds collapsed for the day, their hot wind rushing across the dark mesa. The tall man removed his black baseball cap, wiped sweat from his forehead with the back of his hand, put the cap back on and pulled it down over his eyes.

They were nearly a quarter mile out behind the back of the rundown house.

The agent tried to run, and the tall man was on him in three steps, simply tripped him and let him fall face-first onto the hard desert dirt. He grabbed an elbow and pulled the man to his feet, said don't do that again, and pushed him on.

The trail narrowed. No other people were in sight. No buildings. Just parched earth, a black night with stars above, ringed by the failing clouds that had promised rain but refused to deliver.

They stopped at the edge of a small gully, under a giant, dense mesquite. The tall man pulled a switchblade from his pocket, came up from behind and slit the agent's throat. He gave the dying man a quick shove into the gully and returned to the rundown house to wash the knife.

CHAPTER 7

Like any good swinger, I waited until after ten o'clock, then cruised Pleasant looking for a garage door partway open. It wasn't a random search. I had three addresses to check: The Mack residence, Bo Rollins' house, and Jimmy Mendoza's. The first two were in the country club, where the richer half, and those that wanted to seem that way, lived.

The logic was simple: Among real estate agents in a small town, sparks sometimes fly. When they cross paths socially, the sparks sometimes become flames. When they start sharing lovers, well, I could only imagine. I didn't have many leads to follow on this case, so a lover's den seemed like a good place to start.

The night was sticky. Thunderheads had built all day, teasing the possibility of rain, then flattened out and dissipated in the evening, leaving their moisture hanging in the air like a small bathroom after a hot shower.

I turned the red Jeep Wrangler off Pleasant Way at the gated entrance. A guy named Mike Martinson, who'd helped me zero in on the Bernstein murder a few weeks back, manned the guard shack. Mike and other guards made sure everyone coming in and out of the gated portion of Pleasant was a resident or an invited guest. He came out with his big smile, big teeth, lanky frame and the slight stoop that made him seem older than the twenty-something he was.

"Hey, Mr. Quinn," he said, his hair flopping across his forehead. "Another murder?"

"Not sure yet," I said. "For now I'm just looking for romance. Let me in?"

"You know the rules," he said. "Gotta have permission from a homeowner to get in."

"You heard about Joe Mack?"

"Sure. That realtor who disappeared yesterday. Everybody's talking about it."

"I think he'd say it's OK to let me in." Mike and I had developed trust on the Bernstein case. I had little doubt he'd help me out.

"So you're on the case."

"I am."

"And you're not going to tell me more than I need to know."

"Mike, who's the detective here?"

Mike smiled his goofy smile. "Anything I can do to help?"

"Yeah, actually. And you'll keep it between us?"

"You know me," Mike said.

"The Macks throw a lot of parties?"

"Now and then, sure."

"And anyone who comes to the party has to sign in here at the gate."

"Yep. Unless they live in the country club."

"A list of who comes to his parties would be interesting to me."

"I can't do that, Mr. Quinn. It'd get me fired."

"But if I guessed a name on the list, you could confirm it."

Mike looked both ways. Nobody was around. "No way,

Mr. Quinn. Can't do it. Nope. Sorry."

"Jimmy Mendoza?"

Mike looked up at the sky, looked around, grinned a little.

"Thanks Mike. The other thing you can do is let me in."

"If I do, you won't tell anyone?"

"Pinky swear."

"And you won't shoot anybody?"

"I don't carry a gun, remember?"

"And you won't start any fights?" Mike crossed his arms.

"I can't promise that."

"I read what you did to that drone guy the other day. He's barely alive. Looks like he clocked you a couple times, too." Mike pointed at my face.

"But I'm *fully* alive," I said.

Mike Martinson grinned and the gate went up. "Have a nice evening, Mr. Quinn."

***

My iPhone guided me to the Mack house, the route meandering around two golf courses. There were no cars in the driveway, none at the curb, and the garage door was closed. The lights in the house were on but there was no evidence of a party. I considered knocking on the door, but wanted to learn more about who was swinging with whom before approaching Joanne Mack alone, and before confronting Madison about how much she really knew.

I pulled away and followed the phone's GPS to Bo Rollins' place. The lights were all off and the garage door closed.

I wound my way out of the country club, thanked Mike Martinson at the gate, and headed to Jimmy Mendoza's house.

Right on Inspiration Way, left on Opportunity Trail, wondering who the hell named the streets of Pleasant.

Ahead, a red BMW and a white Infinity were parked across the street and halfway down the block from Jimmy Mendoza's place. The rest of the street was empty. The driveway was empty. Swingers probably didn't want to make it obvious where they were swinging.

Jimmy made up for not living in the country club by having a huge home outside its gates. The two-story, stucco McMansion took up all but a few feet on either side of the large suburban lot. The front yard featured a fake stream, rocky mounds to provide contour, and cacti spaced expertly. Every inch neat and tidy, like Jimmy. The entry was tall, grand, arched and columned. In all, an odd marriage of Southwest and Roman architecture that made people feel even wealthier than they were.

The garage door was open partway, a black Lexus and a black SUV inside. I parked in the driveway and got out.

I slipped under the door, walked through the garage and opened the door into a laundry room. Etta James crooned softly from somewhere deep inside the house. The laundry room opened to a short hallway. I followed it into a large formal dining room with more faux Roman columns and arches, painted to look like marble, cracks and everything. The floor was real marble, but my running shoes made no sound. An oversize dinner table was covered with bowls of chips and dips and plates with the remains of finger foods.

I walked through the dining room into an Emeril-inspired kitchen, all granite and commercial-grade stainless steel appliances. I could hear voices but hadn't seen anyone yet.

An arched opening separated the kitchen from a cavernous living room fit for a toga party. I tucked behind a wall and approached the arch, then emerged partially obscured by a fake, potted tropical plant and leaned a shoulder against the archway. There were three couples in various states of undress. None of them noticed me. As a private eye, it was my job to notice things. So I commenced noticing as much as I could.

Bo Rollins, the former pitcher, wore tighty whities and a Mets game jersey. Bo, all six-six of him, slow-danced with a much younger, well-tanned naked woman whose face was buried in his chest. To be precise, she wore two things. A Mets cap, from which a purple pony tail protruded perkily, and impossibly tall ankle strap heels that raised her just high enough so Bo's hand could reach her ample but shapely alabaster bottom. The fingers of his left hand clutched stark tan lines in what looked to be a curveball grip.

Rollins' frosted-blond wife, in nothing but a pair of sheer panties, a laurel wreath on her head and expensive Scottsdale breasts, held a wine glass by the stem with two fingers. She was well-toned for a woman in her forties, no doubt a product of endless days on tennis courts, in gyms, at spas. She stood chatting with Jimmy Mendoza, who sported a gold chain around his neck, a gold Rolex on his wrist, a gold wedding band on his finger, and a partly erect but not oversized bit of manhood hanging out front.

Jimmy drank beer from a bottle, eyeing the breasts made in Scottsdale. The owner of the breasts smiled and shook them gently from side to side.

Jimmy's nude wife Rachael, a natural redhead, sat on the couch kissing a much younger man I didn't know, presumably Donovan Fisk. He had a naturally curly mop of brown hair reminiscent of Michelangelo's David, biceps to match, and wore a toga tugged up farther than I cared to notice.

Still in my jeans, t-shirt and running shoes, I folded my arms, and tried to grasp the allure of the lifestyle. The view from here, or at least three-sixths of it, wasn't bad, I concluded, but I'd already swung beyond my comfort zone. It was time to stop noticing things, before it became just staring.

I had a plan. It was simple. I'd used it many times before, as a reporter and recently as an upstart private investigator.

When I didn't have any real evidence, but I had some suspicions, I liked to surprise people, then watch their body language for hints of guilt or fear or whatever they might give away in that unguarded instant. It could save a lot of work, actually looking for clues and all that. I'd never employed the tactic with naked people before, so there was a lot to watch for when I said, "Anybody seen Joe Mack?"

Bo Rollins' wife turned away from Jimmy Mendoza and dropped her wine glass. It shattered on the marble floor, red wine pooling around the shards. Bo turned and narrowed his beady pitcher's eyes at me without taking his left hand off the young woman's backside. They stopped dancing but stayed pressed together. She was tipsy on her spindly heels. The big tall leftie tightened his grip on the curveball so she wouldn't fall. She giggled and looked at me, her purple ponytail bouncing around, then her faced dropped. I gave a half grin so Becca would know I recognized her, not enough for anyone else to pick up on it. She buried her head back in Bo's chest.

Jimmy's redheaded wife Rachael and the presumed Donovan Fisk both just froze, wide-eyed.

"What the fuck," Jimmy said, inadvertently aiming his manhood my way.

"Who the hell is he?" Bo said.

I took that one. "Eli Quinn, private investigator."

I liked to be straightforward with people whenever it served me well. If someone in this room knew where Joe Mack was, I wanted that person to know who I was. Make them feel cornered. People do stupid things when they feel cornered.

Jimmy took a step my way, pulled himself up as tall as he could, handed his beer to Bo's wife. His body, dark and shaved save the patch on top and another down low, bulged from years of pumping iron, shined like polished walnut.

Bo's wife took a step back and covered her breasts with her arms in a sudden onset of modesty. Jimmy's wife and the presumed Donovan Fisk disentangled themselves on the couch. She covered herself with two orange pillows that clashed terribly with her hair. Fisk stood up, a good two or three inches taller than me, thankfully let his toga fall back into place as his muscular arms hung to his sides, relaxed, fists clenched tight. He looked even more like the statue of David now. They all looked to Jimmy, while Bo—notorious for beaning batters and starting fights on the field and off— just kept staring at me.

All this I registered in the time it took to push my shoulder off the wall and prepare myself for whatever might come next.

"What the fuck're you doing in my house?" Jimmy said, his erection subsiding. His accent grew stronger as he spoke faster.

"I told you. Looking for Joe Mack."

"That's twice you get in my face," he said.

Jimmy should have thought twice before doing what he did next. But hotheads aren't known for thinking twice.

He came at me the way strong, overconfident guys will, barreling straight in, sans any strategy. I hoped this would be easy. I wasn't in the mood to compound the damage to my body, just as I was recovering, just when I was about to get my first kiss from Sam Marcos. And I really, really didn't want to wrestle a naked man.

I blocked his sloppy punch with my right forearm, grabbed his other arm with my left hand and encouraged his momentum to carry him into the wall. He hit with a loud thud, a full body slam that stunned him without breaking anything. I wasn't out to hurt Jimmy Mendoza. Yet.

I shuffled to the right, careful not to turn my back on the outsized men in the room, an angry pitcher and a sculpture-of-David lookalike. I could handle two men at once, maybe three if I got lucky, but maybe not these three. The statue of David quivered like a dog waiting for a command, squinted, waited. Bo hadn't moved.

Jimmy Mendoza crouched and put fists up like a boxer. Clearly he'd never boxed. He moved in like a snail. I sprang forward like a grasshopper, struck him in the chest with a push kick that put him flat on his back, sliding into the couch, just missing the wine and broken glass on the floor.

I landed on my feet, ready for anyone else who might want to go a round.

The statue took a step forward, made eye contact with me, thought better of it and held his ground. Bo still clutched tan lines, watching me. Etta James finished her song and started another.

"Joe Mack's not here," Bo said. "Nobody's seen him since yesterday."

"So I heard." I looked at Bo, then Jimmy, then their wives, then the statue. "I figured one of you might know where he is."

Bo shook his head once. "Nope." Cool as a relief pitcher in the bottom of the ninth. I was surprised he hadn't come at me. But I was glad. The best fights were usually the ones that didn't happen.

"Why the fuck should we know where he is?" Jimmy regained his wits, rolled over and got up on his knees, keeping an eye on me. I relaxed my stance.

"Joe Mack's the local real estate king," I said. "You guys are what, pawns? Maybe one of you would like to see him gone."

"What's he talking about?" Rachael said, an edge to her voice that comes when a wife hears her husband might be up to no good. "Jimmy, what the heck?"

"Nothing, hon. This guy's a fucking amateur. Doesn't know what the fuck he's talking about." He stood up. Shook his head, glared at me. "You come in here, break up our party. Assault me. Tell me why I shouldn't call the police."

"Correction," I said. "You assaulted me. I was just enjoying the view from the cheap seats. But go ahead and make the call. It'll make for a great newspaper headline.

Jimmy Mendoza beaten up while naked at a wife swap."

"Dickhead," he said. "It's not a wife swap. It's the lifestyle. Idiots like you don't understand."

"No, we probably don't," I said. "Does Joanne Mack understand?"

Jimmy's eye twitched. A yes, according to my detective manual.

Bo let go of Becca Jones' bottom, took half a step my way. She nearly tipped over on her spike heels. Bo hadn't stopped watching me, but now he looked into the middle distance, thinking hard, deciding something. He refocused on me. Donovan Fisk's feet remained frozen, like any good statue, but his head was swiveling between Jimmy and Bo, appearing to search for guidance.

"None of our business what Joanne does," Bo said.

I nodded. "I see." And I *had* seen a lot. More than I needed to. And I'd learned some things. And I was pretty sure I'd made somebody nervous, maybe a couple somebodies. I nodded, turned and walked out the way I'd come in. Jimmy Mendoza cursed at the back of my head as Etta James sang me out.

CHAPTER 8

"You're looking better," my best friend Jack Beachum said. "Stitches out, swelling's down. Still ugly, but better."

"Thanks Beach." I finished the last of my scrambled eggs, wished for one more piece of bacon as I slid the plate away. I dug into a strawberry tart. It was unbearably delicious.

Beach leaned back against the side of the building, his Denver omelet done, and bounced the red rubber ball off the outdoor patio at Lulu's Grind. Solo stopped napping long enough to follow the ball, bobbing his head up and down a few times, until he remembered that Jack Beachum never gave up his rubber ball.

Having recently killed a man, Beach was, per standard procedure, on leave. He wore civilian clothes—flip-flops, blue cargo shorts and a yellow Hawaiian print shirt that clashed with his fair skin and short sandy hair.

"Loudest shirt I ever saw," I said. "A man in his seventies oughta have more dignity."

"Ladies love it," Beach said.

"Your wife?"

"Especially my wife."

I just shook my head and smiled. Over breakfast, my friend had listened to what I knew about Madison Mack, which didn't take much time, and what I didn't know, which was a lot.

"I picked up on some rumors yesterday," I said. "Lot of swinging going on in Pleasant."

Beach nodded, bounced the ball.

I didn't tell him about my adventures last night. Being a lawman, Beach didn't always want to know *how* I knew some of the things I knew. And I'd promised discretion to Aahna Chaudhari, mostly for Becca's sake.

"Joe Mack, Jimmy Mendoza, Bo Rollins. Their wives. All swingers."

"Knew about Mendoza and Rollins," Beach said.

"And how'd you come by that juicy tidbit?"

"I'm posse," he said. "We're aware of everything that goes on in this town."

The posse was a volunteer group within the Maricopa County Sheriff's Office. Posse members, most of them retired cops, wore uniforms almost identical to sworn deputies, drove nearly identical cars. They carried the same crime-fighting gear, and many were allowed to pack weapons. But their duties were confined to crowd control, helping out at school crossings, and other support roles. They were supposed to refrain from making arrests or plunging into dangerous situations, instead calling for backup. Jack Beachum had been a lawman forever, first in Texas, then Scottsdale, and now in Pleasant, and he didn't always follow the posse guidelines.

"Almost everything," I said.

"Didn't know Joe Mack was involved. But Mendoza and Rollins are known hotheads. We keep an extra eye on known hotheads."

"How about a guy named Donovan Fisk."

"Never heard of him," Beach said.

"How come you never told me there were swingers in Pleasant?"

"You didn't need to know," he said, squeezing the rubber ball with his left hand, then tossing it over to his right and continuing to squeeze.

I nodded. Beach and I shared a lot of information with each other. And we hid a fair amount. It was a necessary part of our friendship. When I was an investigative reporter, Beach gave me tips now and then, ran down the occasional lead for me. He'd helped me with my first two cases as a private eye.

I asked him if the investigation into Joe Mack's disappearance, a joint effort by the Scottsdale Police and Maricopa County Sheriff's Office, had revealed anything.

"If it did I shouldn't tell you," Beach said.

"But you will."

"How would I know anything? I'm off duty."

"You still talk to people on the inside," I said. The law was not just a job for Jack Beachum. It was his hobby.

Solo snored. He was used to Beach and me lingering after a meal. A waiter came out, poured more coffee and took our plates. Lulu would be inside on this busy morning, taking orders, clearing tables and helping the cook. We were the only guests braving the growing heat on the patio.

"And what I tell you didn't come from me," Beach said.

"Never does."

"Eyewitnesses confirm Joe Mack was at the Princess that morning. His cell phone records show he took a call at 11:30 from Joanne Mack."

"His wife."

Beach nodded. "Then nothing."

"Joanne know that you know about the call?"

"Yep, guy working the case asked her about it. She said it was nothing, just checking in."

"Anybody see him after that?"

"Not that we could discern."

"They find his car?"

"In the hotel parking lot."

"And no other calls. No texts?"

"Nada."

"His phone just go dead?"

"Dunno."

"That all you got?" I grinned.

"I'm just posse."

"Can a posse guy look into one Donovan Fisk, find out where he lives, what he does, check his priors, stuff like that?"

"Darn tootin."

CHAPTER 9

Madison Mack was on my growing list of people to talk to today. She had some explaining to do. But first I wanted to get a bead on her mother, see if she was as bad as people were saying.

I left Jack Beachum at Lulu's and drove to the country club, rang the doorbell at the Mack residence and waited. Was about to ring the bell again when Joanne Mack opened the door partway. She was barefoot in a terry cloth robe, tied loosely to invite plenty of imagination. Her short hair, blond with dark roots, was wet.

She leaned against the edge of the door, rubbed her hair with a towel in one hand, looked me up and down. It felt like an appraisal. The act of toweling caused her robe to slip open more, revealing most of one plump, expensive breast, which I noticed with my excellent peripheral vision. I kept my focus on her face.

"Well," she said, her voice at the edge of husky, what any heterosexual man would call enticing. "Hello."

"Hi Mrs. Mack. I'm Eli Quinn, private investigator."

She stopped toweling her hair. "And?"

"I wanted to ask you a few questions about your

husband."

"He's not here," she said, voice flat now, toweling again. "He's goddamn missing."

"I know. Your daughter hired me to find him."

"Bitch." She said it softly. I don't think she realized she'd said it out loud. The toweling stopped. Her eyes, green like her daughter's, took on an unfriendly glare identical to the one I'd seen in Madison.

"Madison hired you?"

"Yes ma'am."

"But the sheriff and the police are already looking into it," she said.

"I understand that."

"So what are you doing?"

"Looking into it."

"I don't need you to."

"All due respect, ma'am, your daughter hired me. I'm working for her. I don't need your permission."

"My daughter is not in charge. I am. We don't need you."

"Yes ma'am. May I come in?"

Joanne Mack just glared at me a moment. Then she blinked and made her eyes inviting again, curled the corners of her mouth up ever-so-slightly. She opened the door with a careless flick of a hand, walked toward the back of the house, dragging the towel on the floor. There were two Joanne Macks, and I'd met both of them in less time than it takes to undress.

A prickly feeling on the back of my neck suggested a game had begun. I wasn't sure what sort. I entered, closed the door and followed her.

The floor plan was wide open. I could see from the entryway through the dining room, kitchen, and living room, and on through a wall of windows in a sunken living room that looked out on a kidney-shaped pool, with a spa and rock waterfall. The ceilings were high, the floors were slate, the furniture white leather with splashes of color in pillows and furry blankets.

"Get you a drink?"

"No thanks." It sounded good. The drink. But having one didn't seem like a good idea at all. It was nine-thirty in the morning.

Joanne Mack walked over to the bar, picked up a glass with half-melted ice in it, and poured herself what appeared to be a second scotch while I stood behind her and waited.

"Have a seat, Mr. Quinn."

"Just Quinn." I sat in a white club chair facing an oversized white couch.

"If you were drinking, what would you have?"

"Gin and tonic," I said without hesitation. My mouth watered a little, thinking of the lime.

She took a glass from a cabinet, put ice in it and poured a double shot of Tanqueray, opened a fresh bottle of tonic and topped it off, then cut and squeezed in a wedge of lime. Perfect.

She walked across the room in no rush, her eyes on me. She leaned over and handed me the drink I didn't want, lingered a moment so I could enjoy the view, this time the better part of both costly items. I kept my eyes on hers. They didn't exactly twinkle, but they were active as hell.

She settled on the couch. A glass coffee table separated us. Her robe returned to doing its job fairly well up top, but now it separated around her crossed legs to reveal most of one. I set the drink on the coffee table and returned my focus to her face. I sat on the edge of the club chair, elbows on knees. Didn't plan to be here long. Trained detectives know danger when they see it.

"Have you found my husband?" The enchanting voice still.

"Not yet."

"Do you think you will?"

"That's the plan."

"Have any clues?"

"A few," I said. "Do you mind if I ask the questions now?"

She smiled, nodded for me to go ahead.

"When was the last time you saw your husband?"

"When he left the house day before yesterday, around eight, to go to the conference."

"Anything unusual about him?"

"Like what?"

"I don't know. Nervousness. Rushing. Odd conversation or strange activity. Tea instead of coffee maybe? Fruit Loops instead of Corn Flakes?"

She blew a little air out in a near-laugh, sipped her drink. "No. Nothing I noticed. He finished the pot of coffee before I was up, as usual, and I had to make my own. He was glued to his computer, as usual. Then he showered, dressed, and left."

"No kiss?"

"Is that relevant?"

"Just curious."

"Well, then, none of your business." She took a swallow of scotch and switched to a bored-sounding tone. "But yes, we kissed, said goodbye, yada, yada." She drank her drink, pointed at mine, which I hadn't touched. "Join me, Quinn."

I glanced at the gin and tonic, beads of condensation on the outside of the glass, imagined the taste of it, something like a the smell of pine trees, then blinked to clear my head. "Did you talk to him after that?"

She sighed. "I don't remember. Maybe. I make a lot of calls every day. And by then I was distraught. Not thinking clearly. You understand."

"Of course," I said. "Do you usually talk to your husband during weekdays?"

"Sure, when there's business to discuss."

"Maybe you talked to him a little before noon?"

She paused, just briefly. Her eyes danced. "Yes. I told the

sheriff that. But how would you know?"

I pulled a business card from my pocket and put it on the coffee table. "Private investigator, like I said. We find stuff out."

She nodded with scrunched lips, took another drink.

"What did you talk about?"

"I just called to see how the conference was going," she said.

"And what'd he say?"

"Fine. Everything fine." Her voice was losing some of its lustiness. I was wearing her down. "I told him I loved him and we said goodbye."

"Did you try to call him later?"

"Yes, of course. I was worried sick."

"How many times?"

She pulled her robe closed, like a curtain coming down on a show. Her voice flat now, angry. "Mr. Quinn, I'm not sure I like where you're going with this."

"Where's that?"

"Do you suspect me of something?"

"Should I?"

"Of course not." She finished her drink.

"I'm just asking questions, trying to learn everything I can about what happened."

"Well, I'm fucking offended," she said, hint of a slur. "My husband is missing. I don't know why. It's not like him to skip off, and I'm worried. Now you come in and accuse me of, of, of what?"

"I didn't accuse you of anything."

"Well, good." She slammed her drink down on the glass end table. "Because I just want someone to find my husband."

"We share the same goal," I said. "How many times?"

"What?" Her forehead was a squiggle of confusion.

"How many times did you try to call him?"

"Oh, Christ, I don't know." She waved a hand in the air.

"Three or four. Several. Into the night."

"And he didn't call you? No texts?"

"I haven't heard from him at all."

"Can you think of anywhere he might have gone?"

She shook her head. "No. No idea."

"Has anything been bothering him lately? Money, relationship issues?"

"Mr. Quinn. I've had enough of this. My husband is missing. God knows what's happened to him. I'm out of my mind with worry. The sheriff is looking into it. And you're upsetting me. I think you should go." She picked up her glass, took a drink but realized there was nothing but ice left, and got up to pour another.

CHAPTER 10

The receptionist told me Madison was with a client when I walked into Mack Realty a couple hours later. It was a sprawling operation for Pleasant, with a dozen cubicles and as many private offices.

"She'll see me," I said. What wasn't clear was whether she'd still be my client after this meeting.

"Not if you don't have an appointment." The receptionist was in his late-twenties, neat hair with the front gelled back in a perfect wave, a light blue seersucker sport coat, Sperry Top Siders and a bow tie indicating he had plans to be something but wasn't. "Nobody sees Madison unless I say." He stuck his chin out. I gave him a chuckle.

I called Madison's cell. She picked up on the first ring. No hello. "What can you tell me?" she asked.

"Your receptionist has terrible taste in suits."

"Where are you?"

"Trying to get in to see you. Seersucker here says I need an appointment."

"Last door on the left," she said. She clicked off. Her door opened and she walked out with an elderly man. They shook hands and he made his way out. Seersucker glared at me. I grinned at him and shrugged.

Madison's office was spacious and well furnished. She closed the door, perched on the front edge of a club chair and motioned me to a matching one. I stayed standing, arms folded.

"Strike two," I said.

"What're you talking about?"

"You lied to me again."

"I most certainly did not."

"You must've known your parents are swingers."

She looked away. Her head dropped and her shoulders slumped forward. She took a deep breath and let it out. "I didn't lie to you. I just didn't tell you."

"Same thing in my book."

"Look, Quinn. Being a Mack isn't easy." She looked up at me, most of her composure regained. "My dad is one of the most prominent businessmen in town. Everyone knows him. He is the business. The business is him. My mother is, well, you know…"

"An alcoholic?"

Madison sighed, let her gaze drift up to the ceiling fan that twirled lazily. "Yeah, that too. How'd you know?"

"I paid her a visit this morning."

"She was drunk already?"

"By the time I left, yes."

"She hit on you?"

"Most definitely."

"And?"

"I resisted."

"Wise."

"Would've helped if you'd told me all this before," I said.

"I didn't think it was relevant."

"It's not your job to decide what's relevant. I'm the detective."

"I didn't lie to you."

"You withheld important information."

"Why is their lifestyle important?"

"I don't know yet," I said.

"But you think it is."

"Everything I learn is important until it's not."

"Look, Quinn." Her green eyes were at their warmest, which for Madison Mack was still frosty. She stood, fidgeted with her blazer, folded her arms and looked around the room as if searching for something. Finally she returned her attention to me. "The last thing I need is for people to find out my parents are swingers. It could be the end of Mack Realty."

"Rumors are out there."

"Rumors aren't facts," she said.

"In this case they are."

"But people don't know that."

"Some do," I said.

"Still. You can see how precarious things are right now. And we haven't even talked about the fact that my dad's still missing."

"About that," I said. "You think your mom could have something to do with this?"

Madison jumped back, eyes wide. "Mother?"

I didn't say anything.

"Holy shit. I didn't... I never... I mean, we hate each other, and... but I wouldn't have thought she'd ..." She sat back down on the club chair, slouched, closed her eyes and used one hand to hold her forehead up. "I can't believe she would do something to him. They've been together since high school. Sure, they have their problems, but they still love each other."

"About that," I said. "I had a hunch, looked into it." It's amazing what you can find in public records, in this case on the Maricopa County Superior Court site. "Did you know your mom filed for divorce a couple months ago?"

Madison shuddered. She didn't look up.

"You didn't know."

She shook her head.

"Sorry to be the one to tell you."

She lifted her head. Her eyes were wet. Her lower lip twitched. "You really think Mother has done something."

"Maybe a stretch. But she's on my list of suspects."

"There are others?"

I nodded.

"Who?"

"Not ready to say. But this whole thing is looking ugly. And it'll probably get uglier. To be honest, I didn't want to take the case in the first place. I'm even less enthused about it now."

"You can't stop," she said, wiping an eye and pulling her shoulders back. "We have a deal."

It was my turn to look away. *Eli Quinn, private detective. Doer of good.* I wanted to help people. Madison needed help. She would pay me. And then I could help others. For a dollar, if necessary.

"No more lies?"

"No more lies," she said.

"Three strikes and I'm out," I said.

"I promise."

CHAPTER 11

Three New York strip steaks sizzled in butter in the cast iron fry pan. I sprinkled diced garlic around the steaks and ground some black pepper onto them. Four minutes per side and they were done. Some people needed a recipe for everything, but some of the best meals were just that simple. I slipped two steaks onto plates along with fresh-from-the-garden zucchini, which I'd quartered lengthwise and broiled with a spritz of olive oil and light sprinklings of salt, garlic powder and chili powder.

Sam poured two glasses of inexpensive merlot and waited while I cut the third steak in two pieces and took half of it out through the sliding door into the backyard. Solo followed me out, waited for the command, then devoured his steak in the time it took me to walk back to the kitchen.

"So Eli Quinn went to a swinger party."

"As an observer only," I said.

I'd told her about my encounter with Jimmy Mendoza and Bo Rollins, and their wives, and about their reaction when asked about Joanne Mack. I left out the part about Aahna Chaudhari's secretary and her latest beau, Donovan Fisk.

"I'd heard rumors," she said. "But it's never been more than that."

"Interesting lifestyle," I said.

"Works for some."

"But not us."

"No, not us."

I ate some zucchini. I drank. Sam sipped. "How was the observing?"

I cut into my steak. Took a bite to buy some think time. Finished it with wine. "Parts of it were interesting."

"Mmm-hmm," Sam said. She smiled, picked up a zucchini strip with her fingers and downed it, then went to work slicing her steak.

"You're not a bashful eater," I said.

She shook her head, chewing.

"I like that," I said.

"I like your cooking." She wiped some olive oil from her chin and dove into the steak.

I explained my brief visit with Joanne Mack, the revealing bathrobe, the casual hair toweling. And the parts relevant to the case.

"She wanted to do you," Sam said, cutting her steak a little more vigorously.

"Little question," I said. "And I think she usually gets what she wants."

"Within moments of having met you."

"Seconds, I'd say."

"Bold," she said.

"I *am* rather irresistible."

"No argument there," Sam said. "So what happened?"

"I showed tremendous restraint."

"Was it difficult?"

"Not at all," I said.

"Because you have me."

"A no-brainer."

I told Sam about the divorce filing.

"See? Jealousy, anger," she said.

"And maybe a little retribution on the side?"

"Maybe. Does Joanne seem like the vindictive type?"

"Aren't most people?"

"When they feel wronged," Sam said. "Sure. Most. And a controlling, manipulative personality fits nicely with vindictiveness."

"Which is not the same as murderous."

"But could be," Sam said.

"I love it when you talk psychology." Sam was the best investigative reporter I'd worked with. Better than me. Her stuff matched anything *The New York Times* did, if on a more local level. And her Master's degree in psychology came in handy in her line of work. In turn, it helped me.

I finished my glass and poured another. Sam had barely touched hers.

"I don't know," I said. "All this is conjecture. There's little I know for sure."

"You know Joanne Mack likes sex."

"A lot," I said.

"But that's not unusual," Sam said.

"Unless it's too much."

"How much is too much?"

"You're the psychologist," I said.

"I'm a reporter dabbling in psychology. But I do know that the professional thinking is fuzzy on what qualifies as over-sexed, and what to call it. We used to call such women nymphomaniacs. The modern term is hypersexuality. And of course men aren't exempt, but our culture gives them a pass, doesn't try to attach labels to the male behavior. Anyway, like many aspects of the human condition, there's a continuum."

"No clear good or bad, just differences," I said.

"Right. And the labels aren't always helpful."

"So there's no such thing as too much sex?"

"I think it's like drinking," Sam said. "If it feels good and doesn't hurt you or anyone else, then what the hell. If gets in the way of your life, or if it hurts other people, then it's too much."

I was about to take another drink. I set the glass down. I had no trouble not drinking, until I had my first drink. Then the second, third and fourth came easily.

We finished dinner. Sam helped clean up. I poured the rest of my wine into the sink and felt good about it, promised myself yet again I'd cut back. I went to the slider and let Solo in.

Sam followed, put her arms around me.

Then she kissed me. My lip was still tender and a little swollen, but she didn't seem to mind. I certainly didn't. For years I'd enjoyed the company of Samantha Marcos, as colleagues then friends. We'd danced around the inevitable for months. Those were the thoughts that flitted through my head, along with a brief image of Jess, and then my head was clearer than it had been in a long, long time.

CHAPTER 12

Half a block from the Mack house, I parked at the curb just as the last light of the hot day faded, settling in to see what Joanne Mack might do, if anything. I drove Jess' Jeep Cherokee, which had sat in the garage since her death. I should have sold it, but for whatever reason I hadn't. The Cherokee was white, looked like hundreds of other SUVs in Pleasant. My red Wrangler wasn't so good when I wanted to be invisible.

The lights were on but I couldn't see anything stirring in or around the home. So I waited. Nothing happened, so I tried to think about the case while I waited. Instead, my brain was stuck on Sam.

Our first kiss was one of those moments that resets everything, puts life on a different course. There was before the kiss, and now there was after. I didn't know what was ahead, what we'd do or where it would take us. I just knew, with zero doubt, that we'd do it together. For now, while we'd both wanted more than a kiss, there was something else I had to do. Sam understood. She always understood.

Only a couple minutes had gone by. Still nothing was happening. I turned the Jeep's stereo on and played some

Buddy Guy from my iPhone. Buddy Guy begged me to turn the volume up, but I kept it low, since I was on a stakeout.

We were halfway through Buddy's *Born to Play Guitar* album when the garage door went up and Joanne Mack's white Mercedes backed out. I knew it was hers by the photo of her on the side, and the words *Joanne Mack, Mack Realty*. The windows were tinted and it was dark out, so I couldn't see who was driving. I made an assumption it was Joanne Mack. Sometimes detective work isn't so hard.

I waited until the white Mercedes had turned the corner at the end of the street, then I started the Cherokee and followed. Streetlights did their job well enough that I left my headlights off. With no other cars on the quiet streets of Pleasant's country club section, I stayed well back. The Mercedes' taillights turned right onto the long and winding Country Club Drive. I put my lights on and allowed even more distance between us. She turned left about a quarter mile ahead, so I knew she was not leaving the club section. I sped up, hit the lights, and made the left, just catching a glimpse of her tail lights making a right.

Now I was pretty sure where she was going, so I slowed down. A couple turns later I saw the white Mercedes pull into Bo Rollins' garage. I parked a block away and got out.

***

Technically, breaking and entering is a crime. But if not reported, then it's just another tree falling in the forest. I didn't plan on being reported.

Because I knew some things.

Given his history, Bo Rollins had shown remarkable restraint when I crashed the swinger's party. The towering left-hander, who had one of the meanest, out-of-control fastballs in the majors, beaned more than a few batters during his mediocre Mets career. A batter he hit would come at him, and Rollins would wave him in, invite the fight at the mound.

I was at Shea Stadium in 2004 when Rollins, in his last season, hit Billy Rabb in the shoulder in the top of the first inning, with a fastball that started high and tight and rode in. The same pitch in the fourth hit Rabb in the head. Cleared both benches. Tossed from the game, Rollins walked off smiling. During his playing days, he was arrested twice for disorderly conduct in New York bars. Last year in Pleasant, he punched a guy at the Horny Toad after the guy accused Rollins of hitting on his wife.

And there was Rollins' financial situation. After learning that Joanne Mack had filed for divorce, I dug into some other public records. Nothing surprising about the Macks. But plenty on the temperamental lefty.

Rollins bought his home in the country club for $695,000 in late 2004, just as he left baseball. In 2006, the value had soared to $1.1 million. I enlisted my friend Jack Beachum to search some records I didn't have access to. Beach found that like many people at the time, Rollins took out a second mortgage on the place, then instead of investing it, he'd bought a Hummer, a Harley and a BMW, all in 2006.

In 2008, the housing market plummeted. The market clawed back much of those losses since, but best I could tell, Rollins was still upside-down. He owed more on his home than it was worth. Plus he'd long ago traded in the Hummer and the BMW for newer models, then done so again. His monthly loan payments just on vehicles was about the same as my house payment. His two mortgage payments added up to an unspeakable number.

None of that meant Bo Rollins had anything to do with Joe Mack's disappearance. But it did put him on my short list of suspects. And now one of the other suspects on my list had just parked her car in his garage.

The front door was locked. I went through the side gate and into the backyard.

The backyard was a resort in miniature. Bougainvillea lined the fence. Fountains bubbled. A small waterfall tumbled into the pool. Landscape lighting shined in all the right places.

The slider to the dining room was unlocked, so I went in. It was quiet. Lights were on in the dining room and living room. A pair of woman's heels sat next to the couch, along with a blouse and bra. These people.

I walked through the rooms and down a wide hallway, past three bedroom doors that were closed. Rollins and his wife had two kids, both grown and gone. At the end of the hallway was a double door. I didn't knock.

Sheets flew. Bo Rollins rolled off Joanne Mack. His big white ass bounced off the bed as he sprang to his feet.

Six-six is big.

A wise detective might've had second thoughts about interrupting coitus involving a very large athlete known to have a bad temper, but it was too late for second thoughts.

"God damn you, Quinn," he said. "This shit has to stop."

Joanne Mack pulled a sheet up to her neck, but not before I saw all of what she'd given me a peek at earlier in the day.

"Mrs. Mack," I said, "you have an interesting way of grieving."

"Fuck you, Quinn," she said. The endearment was becoming familiar.

Rollins didn't come at me. I was glad for that. But I wasn't sure why. And I wasn't sure what to do next. So I watched and waited. You can learn a lot by keeping your mouth shut. What I learned was this:

Rollins was flustered. He didn't know what to do. Maybe he was in over his head, probably in more ways than one. Joanne Mack's green eyes were calculating next steps, flicking between me and Rollins. She would take charge. I waited to see which Joanne Mack would do that.

"Bo, sit down," she said it softly, her voice sticky sweet. Rollins stopped glaring at me long enough to pull his tighty whities on. He sat on the edge of the bed, stared at the wall.

"Quinn, you can think whatever you want. Bo and I live the lifestyle. So does Joe. That's between us."

"Certainly was," I said. "Until now."

"With Joe missing, I needed someone to talk to. Bo and I are friends. And, you know," she tilted her head toward him, "one thing led to another."

"It certainly did."

"Again, between us," she said. "Listen, I don't know where Joe is, but I miss him, and I'm confused and upset. He'd understand."

"I certainly hope so," I said.

Bo still didn't know what to do. He looked at the floor, then the ceiling. He rubbed his hands together, squeezed one thumb, then the other. He was a dog on a leash, tail between his legs, but had also spotted a cat he wanted to destroy. It was the first time I'd ever thought of myself as a cat. I decided the whole metaphor was silly. Whatever, Bo's behavior was inconsistent with what I knew about him.

"What you think doesn't matter," Joanne Mack said, her voice shifting to flat, harsh. "And I'm going to tell you right now. We all have reputations in this town, and reputations matter."

"They certainly do," I said.

"To me *and* to you," she said.

"I agree," I said. "My reputation matters to me."

"Then this will be the last we see of each other," she said. "Or I will ruin yours."

"Should I take that as a threat?"

Her green eyes narrowed. I was sure, unlike her daughter, she'd fire some lasers or venom. Instead, she did manage an evil grin. "You certainly should."

Bo Rollins continued fidgeting, staring at the wall.

I let Joanne win this round, gave her a good long stare

and chewed my lip a little, to make it look like I didn't know exactly what was going on, which was pretty much the case. Then I nodded and left.

Let the games begin.

CHAPTER 13

Sleep was blissful, breakfast was big, and my face and body were finally healing from the beating I'd taken in my last case. I had a lot to think about. Sometimes when I had a lot to think about, the best thing to do was not think about any of it. And the best way to escape thought was at Master Choi's dojo. I left home in the Wrangler and headed into the center of Pleasant, past my office, around the central traffic circle where Ringo, the infamous saguaro, stood sentry, then on south down Pleasant Way to the edge of the gridded downtown. I turned right into a more industrial part of Pleasant and pulled up at Choi's Martial Arts.

When Master Choi saw me walk in, he just shook his head. I knew what he was thinking. He'd been telling me not to get into fights, that taekwondo was about staying out of trouble, not getting into it. I worried he might lecture me again. Worse, I feared he might want to spar. Last time we did that I ended up with sore ribs and wounded pride.

It was late morning and the dojo was empty. Master Choi sat on his stool in the corner. At five-five, his feet didn't touch the mat. I bowed, he nodded.

Master Choi sat still and silent as I worked through warmups and stretches, some hard kicks and punches on the bag until I was drenched in sweat, then all my forms from fourth-degree black belt down to white belt, the first one I'd learned as a teenager. For forty-five minutes, my mind focused on my body. And Master Choi barely moved.

I bowed. He nodded. I turned and went to the back of the dojo, to the small room with free weights, and spent thirty minutes doing supersets. By the time I was done I had no energy left, and my body felt better than it had in a week, and my mind was clear. I came back out to find Master Choi still sitting on the stool in the corner.

"You want to fight, must learn how."

"You've taught me well."

"Not show you everything yet," he said. "You not come often. Getting soft. Must come every day."

"I will try," I said. "And you'll teach me more?"

"You come. I teach."

"Thank you Master Choi." I turned and headed off the mat.

"Quinn."

I stopped at the edge of the mat and turned around. "Yes, Master Choi."

"You did a good thing. That man with the drone. Bad man." He was referring to my last case, which had ended with some of the worst taekwondo moves I'd ever used, but they did the trick, and the other guy was still in the hospital. Master Choi slid off the stool, closed his eyes and bowed. I bowed deeply in return.

"Thank you Master Choi."

CHAPTER 14

The silver Camaro, a boxy model from the eighties, was easy to spot, following a couple blocks behind me on Pleasant Way. I'd picked it up soon as I left the office. I turned left onto Pima Road, and so did the Camaro, following a quarter mile back. There were a couple cars between us, but not much traffic. It was easy to tail someone on this six-lane boulevard in the middle of the afternoon, and just as easy to know you were being tailed.

Storm clouds ringed the Valley of the Sun, pregnant with rain that kept not coming, day after day. There was heat. There was moisture. Just not quite enough of one or the other to let it all go. Solo had stayed at the office. I wasn't expecting trouble on this outing, and he preferred the air conditioning to the topless Jeep on sultry days like this. I preferred the topless Jeep, always. I considered looping back to get him, now that I was being tailed, but it was the middle of the day and I'd be around plenty of people, so there seemed little to worry about.

I turned right onto Thompson Peak Parkway, and a moment later the Camaro did the same and re-appeared. In another mile I made a left onto Hayden, and the Camaro stayed with me. I didn't try to lose it. A few minutes later we turned right onto Princess Boulevard, a winding two-lane street posted at fifteen miles an hour. The Camaro backed off but stayed in my mirror.

A moment later I turned the Jeep into the circular entry of the Fairmont Scottsdale Princess, parked off to the side and got out. The Camaro pulled over on the opposite side of the street. I looked at the car, moving my eyes without turning my head, so the driver wouldn't know I knew he was following me. The tinted windows made it impossible to see inside.

There were two guys at the valet, one tall, one short, both in dark brown shorts and light brown shirts. Sweat stained their armpits. I asked the tall one if he was working two days ago.

"Not me," he said. "Jeff was." He pointed with his thumb at the shorter guy, then left to greet some vacationers pulling up. I watched the Camaro out of the corner of my eye. It sat. Nobody got out.

"You here around noon?"

"Yeah," Jeff said. "Why?"

I showed him the photo of Joe Mack on the brochure. "See this guy?"

"Lotta people here that day," Jeff said. "Big convention, you know."

"I know. But I'm only looking for this guy."

The Camaro pulled away. Whoever it was must've figured out whatever it is they wanted to know—maybe that I was, without question, a brilliant detective hot on the trail.

"You a cop?"

"Private investigator."

Jeff looked around. "I'm not sure I should be talking to you."

"Eli Quinn." I stuck my hand out and Jeff shook it. He took the twenty and slipped it into his pocket like a pro. "This guy's missing. His daughter's worried. I'm trying to find him."

"Police already asked about him," Jeff said.

"What'd you say?"

"I said I didn't remember him. Like I said, lotta people here."

"You see anything unusual happen, maybe around noon?"

"Like what?"

"I don't know. Anything out of the ordinary. Maybe someone who didn't fit in. Maybe two guys leaving together, one with a gun to his head?"

Jeff looked up at the clouds for answers. I waited.

"Lotta guys came and went. Some together. I remember there was a van, just before noon or maybe just after, parked right over there." He pointed through some fountains at the center of the circular drive to a trio of black Escalades parked on the other side.

"Mini-van?"

"No. Like the kind electricians drive."

"What was unusual about it?"

"Just sat there a few minutes. Guy didn't get out. I didn't think much of it, but since you asked."

"You see him?"

"Wasn't really paying attention, but I remember he had long hair and a baseball cap."

"How long?"

"Past his shoulders."

"Tied back?"

"No, just loose."

"And you're sure it was a guy."

"Yep."

"What color was the cap?"

"Don't remember. Maybe dark. Blue, black, not sure."

"How was he dressed?"

"Maybe a sport coat or a suit or something. I remember he seemed overdressed for a guy driving a van and wearing a baseball cap."

"Tall, short?"

"Big, I think. Not fat, but not a little guy."

"So what happened?"

"Some other guy came out of the hotel, got in the van, and they left. Listen, I gotta…"

"This guy?" I held the picture out again, another twenty with it. He took the picture, studied it while pocketing the twenty.

"Sorry. Didn't see him. I was busy, and I wasn't really paying attention. I just noticed the van and the driver sitting there. You know, because it was different."

"The guy got in the van, was he tall? Short? Skinny? Fat?"

"Average, I guess. A little stocky."

"Remember what he wore?"

"Not really."

"Think hard, Jeff. Shorts and flip-flops? A Cardinals jersey? Trench coat?"

"Maybe a suit. Not shorts. Like he was at the convention, not on vacation."

"And you're sure it was around noon," I said.

"About then. I got back from break at eleven-thirty."

"Color of the van?"

"Brown, maybe," he said. "Or maroon. Not sure."

"Thanks for your help, Jeff."

"Sure thing."

"Next time, though, pay more attention. I would've tipped you better."

"I'm sorry, sir."

"Just messing with you, kid. Glad you had your eyes open."

CHAPTER 15

Solo licked my face as I woke up on the floor of my entryway, head throbbing. I reached up, felt the lump at the base of my skull. The front door was wide open, heat and humidity pouring over me. Cheek on the cool tile, my fuzzy mind pieced together what had happened.

Solo and I had come home from the office. I was heading right back out to dinner with Sam, so I'd parked the Jeep out front.

Opened the front door, stepped in, Solo barked...

I pushed myself up to my knees, then sat on the floor. My right forearm hurt. I rubbed it. Bruised badly.

Something coming at me. Right arm up reflexively. Darkness.

Solo panted. He looked out the front door, back at me.

"Speak," I said.

Nothing.

"What happened, pal?" I pointed out the door.

He barked. Needles in the back of my head. Glad his habit was the single bark.

I cupped the lump on my head. "Someone attacked me."

Another bark.

"And you attacked him." I pointed out the door again.

Another bark.

"He must've run off, or I'd be dead."

That was obvious. Solo didn't say anything.

"And then you came back to protect me."

He let his tongue loll to the side, equal to a nod. He got a much-deserved head-pat and some serious scratching behind the ears. "Good boy." He licked my face.

Standing up happened in stages. My head cleared as much as could be expected. I pulled my phone from its holster, looked at the time. No more than a few minutes had passed since we'd gotten home.

I called Sam and changed our dinner plans.

***

Sam let herself in my front door wearing a short black dress with spaghetti straps, black heels, a thin silver necklace. Best I could tell that was it. I'd never seen her look more beautiful. Then again, I'd never seen her look less beautiful.

"Hell, Quinn. Our first real dinner date and you cancel last minute. Girl all dressed up." She said it with an upward inflection, hand on hip, and a shake of her dark hair that drove everything else out of my mind for an instant.

"Maybe we can fix that," I said.

She sat on the edge of the club chair, wrapped her arms around my head and gently pulled me into her. She ran her fingers through my hair. I closed my eyes. "I should get hurt more often."

"Don't you dare." She pulled back, looked at me. "You OK?"

"Sore, but yeah. I'm fine."

"What happened?"

"I got whacked in the head."

"You told me that," she said.

"Amnesia?"

"We'll see. If you start asking me things over and over, I'll let you know. Did you see him?"

I shook my head. Gently. Solo sat at my feet, moving his head back and forth as we talked.

"So he broke in?"

"I hadn't locked the slider."

"Not a lot of crime in Pleasant," she said.

"Until recently." I'd solved a murder, figured out who tried to assassinate a state senator, and now this, all before the official start of summer.

"What'd he hit you with?"

"Not sure. A stick. Maybe a bat."

"Maybe a Mets bat?"

"Maybe."

"Jesus," Sam said. "You're lucky, then."

I raised my arm to show her the bruise that was forming.

"You blocked it."

"Partly."

"Good reflexes."

"Master Choi taught me well."

"He must not have known you had Solo," she said.

"Solo's a good deterrent. If Solo'd been at home, the guy would never have broken in."

"Why didn't Solo tear him apart?"

"Not what he's trained to do. Trained to attack on command, but also to protect me."

"So he chased the guy off," Sam said. "Just enough force…"

"And maybe a little more."

"But then he came back to protect you."

"Per his training."

Solo waited patiently. She petted his head and he closed his eyes and leaned into it. I understood. I told Sam I had to call Jack Beachum. Beach picked up on the second ring.

"Beach, I need two favors."

"Hallelujah," my friend said. "At your service."

"See if you can find Bo Rollins."

"And what do I do if I find him?"

"Look for bite marks."

"Come again?"

I told him what had happened.

"You're lucky he's a pitcher, not a slugger," Beach said.

"He never could hit," I said.

"Most pitchers can't."

"You'll look for him?"

"On it," he said.

"And don't tell anyone I'm alive."

"Swinger think you're dead?"

"Might."

"And that gives you an advantage," he said.

"Might."

"You're dead to me," Beach said.

"Thanks. And can you keep an eye on Madison Mack?"

"You suspect her, too?"

"No, but she might be in danger."

"You tell her that?"

"No. I don't know what the hell is going on. We got one missing person. His wife and daughter can't stand each other. The guy looking into it gets smacked in the head. Two of my three prime suspects are sleeping together. Hell, maybe all three of them are. I don't know. But somebody's nervous and stupid things are being done."

"You stirred it up," he said.

"That was the plan."

"I'll get somebody to watch Madison," Beach said. "Nobody'll get near her."

"Thanks Beach. I owe you."

"Let me count the ways."

I laughed. "You get anything on Donovan Fisk?"

"Nothing damning. Twenty-seven, lives in Scottsdale. Rich kid. Dad started and sold some internet thing, made millions. Donovan works at the Troon North golf course in

Scottsdale. One DUI, otherwise no priors."

"Cell phone?"

Beach read the number off and I memorized it, said goodbye and put my phone on the end table. Sam walked to the kitchen. I marveled.

"We should go to the hospital," she said over her shoulder, opening the fridge.

"No we shouldn't."

"Get you checked out."

"I just got out of the hospital."

"As a precaution."

"I'm fine, Sam."

"Beer?"

"Not tonight," I said, surprising myself. Sam took out a Sierra Nevada, popped the top, took a pull longer than any I'd ever seen her take. She came back and sat on the arm of the chair.

"You could've died, Quinn."

"But here I am."

"Sometimes I don't like what you do for a living."

"You got me into it."

"And you're good at it," she said. "But it's dangerous."

"I accept the risk."

"Because it's worth doing. Because it's meaningful."

I nodded.

"I understand that," she said. "And I have to accept the risk."

"Can you?"

"I must."

We sat in silence a moment. Solo decided the excitement was over and the petting had come to an end. He went to the corner of the living room and curled up on his bed.

"You'll stay?"

"I didn't bring anything," she said.

"Maybe you won't need anything."

CHAPTER 16

S am Marcos pressed against me, an arm around my waist, a leg over mine, long black hair spread across my chest. Morning sunlight bounced off the pool, danced in baubles on my bedroom ceiling. Sleep had been long and deep. The sex defied description, confirming all the expectations that had built up over the past year.

I lifted the sheet, saw Sam's perfect backside naked for the first time, acknowledged I was now officially the luckiest man in the world, and shook my head. That hurt. I groaned. Sam woke.

She looked at me with half an eye, snuggled back into my chest. "Eli Quinn," she said. "Goddamn."

"So we can do it again sometime?"

"Forever," Sam said.

She closed her eyes. I closed mine. We lay still a moment.

"You must be hungry," she said. "You didn't eat last night."

"Starved."

"How's your head."

"Hurts."

"How many?" She held up three fingers.

"Six," I said.

"You'll be fine."

Reluctantly, I slid my arm out from under Sam, got up and showered. I dressed, came out and went to the kitchen. Sam was wearing one of my button-up dress shirts, the sleeves rolled up, long muscular legs one-hundred percent on display, scrambling my brain while she scrambled some eggs.

She turned her head. "Toast?"

"You cook?"

"Of course I cook."

"We'll see," I said. "Toast, sure."

She poured a cup of coffee and handed it to me. I wasn't sure what to do. My head hurt, I was hungry, I needed coffee, but most of all I wanted to hold Sam Marcos. I put the coffee on the counter and did the smart thing. She held me back, then she pushed away. "I think you have a killer to go look for."

"Could be a kidnapping," I said.

"Either way."

"Looking less and less like Joe Mack just snuck away of his own free will."

"Still possible," Sam said.

"Three percent chance."

"Two."

"That shirt looks fantastic on you," I said.

"Don't change the subject."

"Will you wear it again some morning?"

"It's becoming a favorite." She put the toast and eggs in front of me. The toast was undercooked, soggy with butter. The eggs were runny, over-salted.

"Delicious," I said through a mouthful. My scrunched face must've suggested otherwise.

"Screw you, Quinn."

"That shirt looks fantastic on you."

Sam smiled.

CHAPTER 17

Jack Beachum and I sat down at Lulu's for breakfast, the second one for me and one I hoped would erase the memory of Sam's cooking. Beach was still in civilian clothes, fire engine red cargo shorts and a clashing peach-colored t-shirt, green socks and black Velcro Tevas.

I put up a hand to shield my eyes from the glare. "Who dresses you?"

"Wife usually signs off before I go out in public. She's out of town a couple days."

"You need to get your uniform back," I said. "Before you cause a traffic accident."

Beach ignored me. "Rollins' wife hasn't seen him since yesterday afternoon."

"You go talk to her yourself?"

"Yep," he said. "Buddy on the posse tipped me off."

"I thought you're not supposed to be doing posse stuff."

"I'm not."

"You think she was telling the truth?"

"Unless she's an excellent liar," he said.

"Lotta people are."

"My five decades of experience in law enforcement gives

78

me a keen sense for bullshit. I'd say she was genuinely worried."

"Your posse sense."

"Exactamundo," Beach said. "I think she's worried there's more going on with her little Bo than she knows."

"I think she's right," I said. "What'd you tell her?"

"That I thought there was more going on with her little Bo than she knows."

"And?"

"Genuine fear in her eyes."

"You'll get a track on their cell phones, check the records?"

"I'm off-duty, remember. Supposed to be like a vacation."

"But you're on it."

"I got a guy coordinating with Scottsdale Police. Need a warrant or some crap like that. Shouldn't be a problem. He calls anybody, we'll know where he is."

"And you'll tell me."

Beach just rolled his eyes.

"Hey also, I need Donovan Fisk's cell."

"I gave that to you last night," Beach said.

I remembered the call with him from last night. All of it. Except the phone number. I could have worried about that, but I had plenty of other things to worry about.

"I forgot it."

"You never forget things," he said.

"Was bonked on the head, remember?"

"And you didn't go to the doctor."

"No need. I'm fine. Doc would've just told me to sit out a few plays. Can't do that right now."

Beach nodded, gave the rubber ball a good squeeze. "You'll tell me if this happens again. The forgetting."

"Will if I remember," I said.

Beach sighed. He pulled a notepad from his hip pocket and gave me the number and I memorized it again. He leaned forward and drank some coffee. Leaned back and bounced the ball off the patio. "I got something else for you. Remember I said there was no activity on Joe Mack's phone after the 11:30 a.m. call? Well, turns out the digital forensics guys dug deeper into the carrier data and were able to figure out where Joe went."

"That'd be helpful," I said.

"You think? Phones are always pinging towers, so these guys don't need you to use your phone to figure out where you've been. Just takes some arm-twisting to get the data from the carriers."

"Privacy," I said.

"Right. Anyway, Joe Mack left the hotel and went through Cave Creek, then on out into the desert, apparently."

"Apparently?"

"Went beyond reach of most cell towers."

Most people thought the cops could pinpoint a person's location from cell phone data. The technology was not that accurate, unless you used GPS records from a phone that used location services. On the other hand, a person didn't have to make a call or text for their general location to be discovered. Accuracy was the problem. In rural areas, a phone might be in range of only one tower. The data can't be triangulated, and would reveal just a big circle of possibility. In this case, Beach explained, it became a cone of possibility, "and no way to know how far the wide end stretches."

"Can I see this cone?"

Beach pulled a folded envelope from his shirt pocket and slid it across the table. "No," he said. "I can't share stuff like that without permission. Heck, I can't even *have* stuff like that given my current status."

I nodded. "Sheriff search this cone?"

"Yep. Helicopters, some door to door. Zippo. Like I said, a big area."

I scratched my head. There was a lot of information on this case, but none of it adding up to anything yet. I thought about Joe's wife. I'd asked Beach to find out how many times she'd tried to call her husband the day he disappeared. "What about Joanne Mack's calls?"

"She called him around 11:30 a.m., like I said. Since his phone seemed to go dead, there's no record after that. But from her records we found she tried him again around 1 p.m., but he didn't pick up."

"That's it? One call?"

"Yep," he said.

"Doesn't sound like a worried wife to me."

"Nope."

"She told me she'd tried calling him several times," I said. "She lied to me."

"Shocking."

"She call anyone else that day?"

"Bo Rollins. Twice. Once around 11 a.m., again around 2 p.m. Couple short conversations."

I nodded.

"Sheriff investigators don't know what to make of all this," Beach said. "But that'd be what I call a clue."

"Indeed."

***

Pleasant's Number Three real estate agent, Jimmy Mendoza, was sitting behind his desk in a windowed office down the hallway. I walked past his secretary, who tried but failed to stop me. Jimmy saw me coming and stood. I let myself in and closed his door.

"You again," he said. He stood straight, eyes narrowed, trying to look tough but lacking the bravado I'd seen before. Happens when you beat a man and he knows you can do it again.

"Probably see a lot of me," I said. "Until I figure out

what's going on."

"I told you, I got nothing to do with this. I don't know where Joe Mack is. I haven't seen Joanne since Joe disappeared."

"Somebody tried to kill me last night. Know anything about that?"

"What? You're kidding?" The slight accent was more pronounced.

I considered telling him about the weapon, but I still wasn't sure who all was involved in what, so I kept that to myself for now.

"You seen Bo the last couple days?"

"No. Haven't seen him since the night you, ah…"

"Saw you."

"Right. Why, you think Bo did something?"

"Crossed my mind. You're on my list, too."

"Look, man, I told you. I didn't do nothing."

"How do I know that?"

"I was at the conference all day. Several agents saw me. I can give you a list."

"I'll take that list," I said. "Have your secretary email it to me this afternoon. Names, phone numbers."

"You call around, start asking questions, I start losing business."

I shrugged. "Get me the list. Help me out. Maybe I don't need to call them. How long Bo and Joanne been sleeping together?"

Jimmy stared at me, hands on his hips.

"Two ways this can go, Jimmy. One way is you help me. You know how the other way goes."

He looked down. Took a deep breath. "We don't talk to outsiders about the lifestyle. Isn't cool to do that."

I waited. He looked up at me, then over my shoulder, then back at me.

"It used to be just getting together, fooling around in a safe place where we all knew where everyone was. It was supposed to be just about sex. I love my wife. Joe loves Joanne. I know he does. But Bo and Joanne started getting serious."

"When?"

"Few months ago," he said.

"What'd serious look like?"

"Joanne was drinking too much. More and more. Joe and Joanne would fight when it was time to leave. Sometimes Joe would go home, Joanne would stay."

"Your place?"

"My place. Bo's place. We all knew what was going on. I don't know how Joe put up with it."

"Joanne is persuasive."

Jimmy nodded.

"Bo have money problems?"

"Bo's a fuckup," he said. "Fun to hang out with. But he blows his money on cars, women, booze. Living the life."

"And the lifestyle."

Jimmy shrugged. "Doesn't make him a killer."

"Bo in debt?"

Jimmy hesitated. I gave him an expectant look to remind him what happens when I don't get answers. Jimmy looked at the floor. "Up to his eyeballs," he said.

"Doesn't invest?"

"Has some piece of shit bar in Cave Creek, rents it out. But otherwise, no."

"What about Joanne?"

"What about her?"

"She got any reason to want her husband out of the picture?"

"I dunno. Maybe. Jeez. You think Bo and Joanne killed Joe?"

"Thought crossed my mind," I said. "Would Joanne want the business?"

"Jeez, I dunno. I mean, she can sell houses, but Joe runs the business."

"And with Joe gone?"

Jimmy thought about that. "Joanne gets the business."

"But she can't run it," I said.

He shook his head. "Probably thinks she can. Maybe she'd bring Bo in."

"Can he run it?"

"Hell no," he said.

"But he probably thinks he can."

"Probably. Egos are big in this business."

***

Joanne Mack opened her door and took a quick step back, eyes wide. "Quinn?"

"Surprised?"

"No, I, um...." She regained her composure as swiftly as she'd lost it, brought her voice down an octave, all business. "I thought I told you to leave me alone. We were clear about that."

"That was before your lover tried to kill me."

"What are you talking about?"

"I think you know. Seen Bo?"

"As a matter of fact, no," she said. "I haven't seen him since yesterday afternoon."

"How's business doing?"

"I don't know. I haven't been into the office for a couple days. I have other things on my mind. Have you found my husband?"

"I'm waiting for you or Bo to tell me where to look."

"Fuck you, Quinn."

"That seems to be the prevailing sentiment," I said. "Should I come in for a drink?"

"No, you shouldn't. If you find Joe, please let me know. Otherwise leave me alone."

If I were a cop, Joanne Mack would probably be detained for formal questioning by now. But I wasn't in the business of arresting people. My job was to find her husband, dead or alive. The odds I'd find him alive weren't looking so good.

She closed the door. I said "Thank you," and left.

***

I called Donovan Fisk from the parking lot outside the Troon clubhouse, introduced myself.

"How'd you get my number?" He had his angry voice on.

"I'm a crack detective."

"I'm working. I can't talk." I could tell he was cupping the phone, not wanting someone else to hear.

"I'm in the parking lot," I said. "You can come out here, or I'll come in there."

Less than a minute later the lanky statue with the floppy curls was standing in front of me in a sky blue polo shirt with a Nike logo on the pocket, expensive tan shorts, lecturing me about what I could and couldn't do.

"Donovan," I said. "Keep your pants on." That made me laugh out loud. "Sorry. Pun not intended. But listen kid…"

"Don't call me that."

"Donovan, you're about two, maybe three words away from getting hit so hard you'll never forget it. I'd suggest you just shut up and listen, then answer a few questions for me."

"I don't have to do shit."

I punched him once just under the ribs, hard enough to knock the wind out of him, not so hard as to cause any permanent damage. He doubled over and made wheezing sounds. I took the opportunity to talk while he couldn't.

"I don't figure you for anything, OK? But you're hanging around with some folks I don't think you should be hanging around with, and I'm smelling a murder in this hot muggy air, and that makes you a possible accessory to murder."

That wasn't true, but I hoped it would scare him and get him talking. Soon as he was able.

"Did you know anybody besides Becca before you went to that party?"

He shook his head, body still bent in half.

"Hear them talk about Joe Mack at all?"

He held a finger up. I waited. And waited.

He took a breath, then another, levered himself up to standing. He spoke in labored bursts. "You're not. A cop. Why ... should I talk ... to you?"

I'd hit him a little harder than intended. "For starters, there's more where that came from." I pointed to his gut. "More important, you don't have a choice. Either you talk to me, or I go to the cops, tell them what I know. They'll pick you up, fingerprints, news, all that." Again, probably not true, but I had him blinking rapidly now, some sort of rich-kid fear response.

"I didn't do anything," he said.

"That's not an answer to my question."

"You'll keep me out of this?"

"If you didn't do anything wrong."

"OK, yeah, after you left." Donovan nodded, as though he'd just delivered a tip.

"You can do better than that," I said.

"OK, yeah. Well, Jimmy, the short one with the hot redhead wife, he asks the ballplayer what's going on with Joe Mack. Ballplayer tells him to fuck off, he don't know. Jimmy's pissed now. Told me and Becca to leave."

"And you did?"

"Fast as we could."

"After putting your clothes on."

"Look man. Yeah, OK, it was kinda weird. But Becca's into it, so I went along."

I didn't care about his sexual tendencies. But he was talking normally now, not hiding anything. Donovan Fisk had just all but crossed himself off my suspect list.

CHAPTER 18

Park Realtors was at the northeast edge of Pleasant's gridded business district, on a street that put it at a disadvantage in terms of foot traffic and visibility. The door creaked when it opened, mini-blinds flopped and slapped when it closed.

A stout woman, maybe early sixties, sat at a desk. Two long dishwater-blond braids draped over a red checkered shirt. I assumed jeans and cowboy boots were under the desk. Behind her were three identical empty desks, an empty office and an empty conference room. She signed papers, turning them over onto a pile. She glanced up over her reading glasses and said good afternoon, returned to signing.

"Everyone must be out selling houses," I said.

"Everyone is just me, Mr. Park and Bo Rollins."

"I'm looking for Bo," I said, trying to sound friendly.

"So am I." Head down, signing away. "If you see the playboy, tell him I've got two calls for him and some papers to sign."

"Doing my best," I said. "When did you see him last?"

She stopped signing, peered over the glasses.

"Who the heck are you?"

"Eli Quinn, private investigator."

"Oh, I know you," she said. "You're that one on the news."

"That's what I hear. I haven't seen me."

"You done good," she said. "Kicked some cowboy ass."

I nodded. She was referring to my last case. I hoped people would stop doing that soon. Then again, it got people talking, and I was in the business of getting people to talk.

"Name's Daisy," she said. She reached out and we shook hands.

"My pleasure, Daisy."

"What's Bo done now? 'Nother bar fight?"

"Something like that."

She waved her pen in the air and looked back at the documents. "He was here yesterday, early afternoon. Pissy mood. Grabbed some files and left. Haven't seen or heard from him since." She went back to signing.

"He say anything?"

"Not even hello. He can be a surly one."

"Know what the files were?"

"No sir."

"I hear he owns a dive bar somewhere. You know anything about that?"

"Buffalo Hide," she said. "It's in Cave Creek."

"Bo run the bar?"

"He rents it out." She signed the last page. Turned it over and put the pen down, picked up the stack and shuffled it into order. She turned her attention to me. "Bar business belongs to Clive Walker. He rents the building from Bo. Walker's behind on rent. I probably shouldn't have said that." She smacked the stack of paper against the desk one last time to flush the pages.

"But you did."

"Slip of the tongue," she said. "Bo gets under my skin a little."

"Tell me more."

"That doesn't seem like a good idea."

I turned slightly and bent down, showed her the giant lump at the base of my skull. "Bo gets under my skin a little, too."

"Bo done that?" Her eyes were wide.

I nodded.

She looked around, as if there might be someone else in the office. "I don't want to get fired."

"If things go my way, there'll be an opening at Park Realty soon. And it won't be yours."

She sighed deeply, then spoke quickly.

"I handle paperwork around here. Bo has me deposit checks for him. You know, when he gets a commission. Which isn't often. And when Walker pays him. Which also isn't often. I think he just likes having people do things for him. It's not part of my job, but there's not a lot going on." She spread her hands to emphasize the empty office.

"How behind?"

"Usually a month or so. But I haven't cashed a check in three months. Maybe Bo's cashing them. But I'd bet my boots Clive Walker's on the verge of bankruptcy. You been to the Buffalo Hide?"

"Haven't had the pleasure," I said.

"It's a dump," she said. "I mean, Cave Creek has some dives, but a dive can have personality. The Buffalo Hide's got nothing going for it. Food's mediocre. Burgers, even. Lousy beer selection. You got to have craft beers today. Surprised it's made it this long."

"And there you go, Daisy, telling me more stuff you probably shouldn't."

"Honestly, I thought you might be here looking into that. Something screwy going on between those two."

"Tell me more."

"Walker's been in three times the past week. More than I saw him the past year. They were in the conference room the other day, shouting about something."

"You hear what they said?"

"Nope. Something to do with money, though. I heard that much. And if I know Bo, probably something stupid."

"People can be stupid with money," I said.

"Especially Bo."

***

Follow the money. I'd learned it as an investigative reporter, and it was the right path more often than not. In this case, it was the only path I had in front of me, so I took it. First I swung home to get Solo. Jack Beachum called as I pulled into the garage.

"Got phone records for Bo Rollins," Beach said. "He was in Cave Creek last night."

"Let me guess," I said. "Buffalo Hide?"

"What's that?"

"Some bar he owns."

"I dunno," Beach said. "I'm just looking at a circle on a map. Doesn't tell us exactly where he was, but narrows it down."

"Just the one call?"

"Yep," Beach said. "Nothing since."

"Even Bo's probably smart enough to turn his phone off, get a throwaway."

"Maybe," Beach said.

"Email me the map?"

"It's in your inbox, as the kids would say."

"OK good. I'm on my way there."

"Need backup?"

"Solo's with."

"Helluva dog," Beach said. "Not the same as a gun."

"Don't start."

"We saved your ass last time. Me, my gun and Solo."

"I can't ask you to come with me, Beach. You're

suspended."

"I'm on leave. Besides. You could ask."

"Come with me?"

"Can't," he said. "But you could swing by, borrow a gun from me."

"Do we have to do this every time?"

"Sure as shootin'."

"Figured. I'll say it one more time. Not gonna carry one. And by the way, thanks for the tip. I owe you one."

My friend just laughed.

CHAPTER 19

A small flock of Harleys huddled outside the Buffalo Hide. Two cars around by a side entrance, probably staff. A dust devil swept the dirt lot, swirling candy wrappers and plastic shopping bags. The bar was straight out of the Old West, with wide vertical board-and-batten siding, a wooden walk with rough-hewn posts and railing around three sides.

Thunderheads towered to the north, one forming an impressive anvil on top. Somewhere, soon, it'd dump a month's worth of moisture in less than an hour, while five miles away not a drop would fall. Monsoon storms were the most capricious nature had to offer.

I pulled into the parking lot and picked from many open spots. I hopped out and headed for the door, Solo at my heel.

It was dark inside, the way a small tavern should be. The walls were plastered with old metal signs, a cow skull with horns, and framed photos in black and white and faded color. The Harley riders, sitting in a booth in the corner, weren't Hells Angels. These suburban bikers had perfect, shiny leathers, Oakley sunglasses and pressed jeans. I was glad. I could mostly factor them out from whatever might happen.

Solo's nose went straight to the ground when we walked in. Working.

The bartender, skinny in a white tee with black hair cut short except for the front hanging over his eyes, was wiping the bar, perhaps a habit rather than necessity. All seven stools were empty.

Above the bar was a photo of an old silver Camaro. I recognized it instantly.

The bartender looked up nervously through his hair with large eyes that darted around the room before zeroing in on Solo. "No dogs," he said.

"This one's OK," I said. I waved a Jedi hand at the bartender but it didn't seem to work.

"No dogs means that one, too," he said, pointing at Solo.

A couple of the Harley riders looked over, then they went back to their conversation. I changed the subject. "You Clive Walker?"

"Nope. Just the bartender. Clive's not here."

"Know where he is?"

"Nope. What about the dog?"

"What about him?"

He looked up, sighed with exasperation. "Like I said. No dogs."

Solo licked my hand. He rarely interrupted me. "What?" He sniffed the floor some more, did a circle, followed a trail over to the bar stool on the far right. He barked once, then sat and growled so quietly I might've been the only one who heard it. The Harley riders went quiet.

I pointed at the bar stool. "Bo Rollins been here?"

"How the hell you know that?" The bartender stopped wiping.

"Meet Solo, world's greatest K-9 private eye."

"And you are?"

"Eli Quinn, humble human private eye."

The bartender's eyes wandered around, then he resumed wiping the bar. "Whaddya want?"

"Looking for Bo and Clive."

"Don't know nothing," he said, eyes following the rag.

"Whose Camaro?"

He blinked, just once.

"Been following me?"

His lip twitched, and he wiped the bar some more.

"Where is it, around back?"

"Like I said, I don't know nothing."

I moved in, sat on a stool, leaned on my elbows. Our noses were a foot part. I spoke quietly and slowly. "Maybe you know a little. Maybe you know a lot. But I know you know something. And so far I don't like your attitude, and neither does Solo. Let's change that, so nothing bad happens."

"Look, asshole," he pointed a finger at me.

I grabbed his thin wrist. Solo barked once, shattering what had become a silent room. The bartender tried to pull back, and neither of us moved an inch. He tried again to slip the grip, and I held firm. The bikers stayed put.

"I figure Bo had you follow me. Or maybe Clive. I'm not after you. But I will be, you don't tell me what you know."

The bartender nodded, put his free hand up. I let go and he raised that hand, too.

"Put your hands down," I said. "This isn't a stickup. Just need to ask some questions."

"OK, man, whatever."

He wiped some more and reached down behind the bar with his right hand. I knew what was coming so I leaned forward. As the gun came up, before it was even pointed at me, I reached in with both hands, grabbing his forearm with my left and his wrist with my right. I moved left and pulled him to the right and forward, slamming his ribs into the bar. I heard the air whoosh out of him and he gasped. His grip relaxed and the gun fell to the floor next to me. I kicked it over toward the bikers. Solo had moved around to block the bartender's only escape path. He sat quietly awaiting further developments.

I'd done the move a thousand times in Master Choi's dojo. Never with a real gun or a real adversary. My nerves were steady but adrenaline surged. I took a deep breath, then gave the bartender a tip while he caught his breath. "Next time have your finger on the trigger when you bring the gun out, and move back a little. You were too close to me. Made it easy."

He gave a feeble nod, clutched his ribs.

"When was Bo Rollins here?"

"Last night, maybe nine o'clock. Had one drink and left."

"He talk to Clive?"

"Yeah. They went in back." He nodded his head to the side, toward the hallway leading to the restrooms with a door in back marked *office*. "I didn't listen."

"They argue?"

The bartender looked down. I waited.

"I'll get in trouble."

"You'll get in more trouble if you don't help me."

He sighed. "Yeah, they argued."

"But you couldn't hear them."

He shook his head.

"When's the last time you saw Clive?"

"They left together last night. I opened by myself today. Just me and the cook." He thumbed toward the kitchen behind him. "Seriously man. Clive made me follow you, wanted to know where you went and what you did. I do what he says. But that's it. I don't know what's going on."

"Thanks," I said. I put my business card on the bar along with two twenties. Madison Mack would reimburse me, so I was liberal with the bills. "Either of them comes back here, you call me. I'll find out either way, but I want to find out from you. Understand?"

"Yeah."

I didn't believe him, but also didn't think the bartender knew much, and I'd done enough threatening. I turned to leave and spotted a photo on the wall, hanging over a booth. Walked over for a closer look. Good-sized man with long hair standing next to an older, dark red Ford Econoline van. I pointed at it. "Clive?"

"Yeah."

I went back and put another twenty on the bar. "Call me," I said. "I have a bunch more of these."

CHAPTER 20

When she called this time, the tall man resisted. He'd done what he agreed to do, thought their deal was done. And this job was riskier, an abduction in broad daylight. They argued. She was persuasive. She offered him more money. And she reminded him he had little choice, given his situation, the leverage they had on him. This target was starting to figure things out, asking questions. Besides, she said, you enjoy doing this, don't you? He didn't argue.

Knocking the man out was easy, a swift blow to the back of the head with the short pipe as he came out of his office. He picked the man up easily, plopped him in the van and slid the door closed. The whole thing had taken less than a minute. No one had seen. No blood, no evidence.

He bound the man's wrists and ankles with zip ties, wrapped his mouth with duct tape, and drove out of Pleasant.

As he pulled up to the house, dust kicked up across the mesa, racing left to right. The wind pulled the driver's door open with a slam. A tumbleweed rolled across the driveway. The clouds to the north were darkening, moving closer, obliterating the sun. Flash lightning lit the darkest cloud, thunder crackling a few seconds later.

He got out, put a key in the padlock and opened the door of the storage shed, an old, empty, simple wooden structure from Home Depot. He went back to the van, slid the side door open, and hoisted the man over his shoulder. The man stirred, but with his mouth taped, hands and feet bound, he was harmless. Back in the shed, he dropped the man on the plywood floor. The man looked up, his eyes wide with fear.

The tall man pulled his cap down over his eyes, closed the door, locked the shed and went over to the house. He'd wait until dark to take the man out to the desert, kill him same as the last one. Sheriff's helicopters had been flying around Cave Creek and out over the mesa the past couple days. And his father was making him nervous. The old man, hearing and sight failing, didn't get out of his chair much. But he'd caught his father watching him from the window a couple times. The tall man had killed several men over the years, but no matter how estranged he felt from his father, down inside he loved him and would never hurt him.

One day his father would die, and the tall man would inherit the ranch. He'd sell it then, make enough to retire on. But his father wouldn't sell now, so they were both dirt poor and the bills were piling up. He was doing what he had to do.

He went into the small, dark living room where his father was watching a soap opera on the old RCA, rabbit ears with foil providing fuzzy reception. Once this deal was done, he'd have a little spending money. He'd buy his father a new TV. Maybe not 4K, but at least something bigger, wall-mount, see about getting a satellite dish.

He thought about the other man that was asking questions, wondered if there'd be a third one to kill. Then he settled in to watch the soap.

CHAPTER 21

Cliven T. Walker had been a Marine corporal, honorably discharged with a Purple Heart thirteen years ago. While in Fallujah, Iraq, his unit came under attack. Walker killed two men in hand-to-hand combat, then was shot in the arm, but still managed to pull an injured Marine back to their bunker. Tough SOB. As he went out for a second wounded man, a grenade exploded and knocked him unconscious.

I learned all that on Military.com. Meanwhile, the coffee maker sputtered and coughed. I got out of my incredibly comfortable office chair, walked over to the counter and poured a cup. Solo, curled up on his dog bed in the corner, yawned wide, then opened one eye, made sure there was no food in the picture, and closed it. On the high, open-beam wood ceiling, footsteps clacked from the hair studio above. My refurbished office, rented from Aahna Chaudhari, was still new to me and I hadn't gotten used to the clacking. But I liked the open space and the mismatched furniture I'd mashed together. The new album from the Buena Vista Social Club played softly on the Bluetooth speaker next to the coffee pot.

Coffee never tasted as good in the afternoon as it did in the morning, but it was just as necessary. And it helped me think. I paced the ten feet from the coffee maker to my desk and back. There was nobody else in my office, which I'd opened only a few weeks back. No other clients beating a path to my door. I chose to see this as a glass-half-full thing, a lack of interruption that allowed me to focus.

Here's what came to mind: Joe Mack had been missing five days—too long to logically be anything but kidnapped or killed. It was easy to assume Clive Walker had something to do with the mystery, but there were plenty of unconnected dots. My suspect list still included Jimmy Mendoza, Bo Rollins and Joanne Mack.

There hadn't been any ransom request, so a kidnapping was gradually ruling itself out. There were other possibilities—maybe Joe did run off with someone and kiss his family and business goodbye, or maybe he went for a mid-day drive into the mountains and accidentally went off a cliff—but given everything else that had happened, including the clubbing of my head with a baseball bat and the disappearance of Bo Rollins, I put the odds of murder at ninety percent, leaving open the slight possibility that he was alive, maybe tied up or locked away somewhere, for reasons I couldn't imagine.

I rubbed my neck, still sore, sipped some coffee, then sat back down. I put my coffee on the desk, pulled my laptop to my lap, propped my running shoes up on the desk and went back to researching.

Clive Walker, hero, returned to a world that probably seemed as foreign as the one he'd been shipped off to. There was a ceremony at the statehouse in Phoenix, then Walker was cast back into society. In 2005, less than a year after his return, he served six months in jail for knifing a man to near-death over a bet on a billiard game in a bar. A year later he was implicated in a murder—a prominent businessman in Scottsdale had his throat slit—but never charged. He held a series of odd jobs—none more than a few months—until 2008, when he began renting a joint in Cave Creek from Bo Rollins and opened the Buffalo Hide. He was arrested and released twice for assaulting customers, and picked up one DUI and served a week for resisting arrest. It appeared he'd stayed on the right side of the law the past twelve months. Appearances can be deceiving.

Clive had almost no family. His mother and sister had died in a car accident when he was a teen. His father, Thomas, would be in his eighties. Clive had never married. None of that meant much. Then the county tax records yielded a genuine clue. Walker's father owned ten acres in the desert out beyond Cave Creek, smack in the middle of Joe Mack's cone of possibility.

***

Just as I was closing my laptop, Solo stood up and moved between me and the office door. Then the bells on the door clanged.

Madison burst through the door with Jimmy Mendoza's wife, the redheaded Rachael, who was dressed much more practically than the last time I'd seen her. Or to put it bluntly, she was dressed.

Madison was out of breath, hair a mess, suit wrinkled. The strap of her small purse had nearly swung off her shoulder and she readjusted it. She looked a couple years older than she did two days ago. Rachael's eyes were red-rimmed and wet. Solo went back to his dog bed and curled up. He knew when he was needed, when there was nothing he could do.

"We can't find Jimmy," Madison said.

Of all the things she might've said, that wasn't on my most-likely list. I tried to process the development. It didn't make any sense. I blinked, ran my fingers through my hair and laced them behind my head.

"Well?" Madison said.

"What do you mean, *can't find?*" I asked.

Rachael wiped her eyes with a crumpled tissue. Madison did the talking. "Rachael was supposed to meet him for lunch. He didn't show. She called and texted him. Nothing. So she called me."

Rachael finally spoke up. "Jimmy didn't do anything. Madison knows him. He wouldn't hurt anyone."

I raised an eyebrow at that. He'd tried to hurt me. Just didn't succeed. Jimmy was a hothead. No doubt about that. But so far he hadn't done anything to make himself out as a kidnapper or a killer. But I had a firm rule that had served me well over the years: remain skeptical until there's proof otherwise.

"I tried calling him," Madison said. "It went straight to voice mail. I went to his office. His car was in the parking lot behind the building, where he usually parks. Secretary said he'd left an hour ago."

"He leave *with* someone?"

"She said he was by himself, thought he'd taken his car," Madison said. "She was surprised when I told her it was still in the parking lot."

I looked at Rachael. Tears were starting to spill. "Jimmy usually good about calling or texting you?"

She nodded vigorously. "Always," she said.

I took a deep breath and pondered that.

"I know what you think about our lifestyle, Mr. Quinn. But Jimmy and I are in love. He would never run off on me. He's a good man."

I nodded. I even believed her. But I still didn't understand what the hell was going on.

"Well?" Madison said again. "Are you just going to sit there?"

I stood. It was the best I could do while I thought. I rubbed my neck and put on my best thinking-hard face by looking up into the corner of my brain. All I knew for sure was that my third case had become much more than the mess I feared stepping in. If Jimmy Mendoza really was missing, and it seemed logical to assume for the moment that he was, then either he got nervous and bolted like an accused man would, or the suspect list in the disappearance of Joe Mack had just gotten shorter and the victim list longer. But that didn't bring the case any closer to resolution. The only clear next step was to find Clive Walker.

"I had the posse keeping an eye on you," I said to Madison, as I moved out from behind my desk. "I assume one of them is outside somewhere. Lock the door and don't let anyone but him in."

"I lost him when we left Jimmy's place," Madison said. "Figured it was you put him up to it. You think I'm really in danger?"

"I don't know what the hell is going on. But people keep disappearing. There's one guy who looks to be in the middle of all this. I'm gonna go find him."

"And find my father," Madison said. She crossed her arms.

I stared at her. Nothing to say to that. Her lips twitched, just once. She knew what I was thinking. Neither of us needed to say it. I nodded once.

"You going to tell me who this one guy is?"

"No," I said. If I knew one thing about investigations, it was to tell people only what they needed to know, when they needed to know it. Madison had a temper, and I didn't need to fuel it. She'd shaken a tail, she packed a gun. I'd learned something about her: She got things done. Right now, I didn't want her doing anything. "Information can be dangerous," I said.

"What if I insist?" she asked. "You *are* working for me."

"I'd refuse. Now we can stand here and argue, or I can go do what you're paying me to do."

"OK." She sighed. "But I don't need protection." She

patted her purse.

I nodded. "You know how to use it?"

"Of course. You still think I'm an idiot?"

I hadn't thought that, not even at the outset. And once we'd gotten past her initial lie, I'd found her to be far from idiocy. *Savvy* would be how I'd describe her. And maybe a little frosty.

"Not one bit," I said.

CHAPTER 22

We rolled into Cave Creek fifteen minutes later. The heat and humidity were suffocating. Thunderheads roiled, their white cotton tops impossibly high, swelling and merging and darkening the sky beyond the town. Lightning flashed and flickered far off. Wind kicked up in gusts. I thought of putting the Jeep top up but didn't want to waste any time. We passed through town and headed out the other side.

The cloud bottoms ahead turned from gray to eerie green. A bolt split the sky in two and snaked into the mountains, the rumble of thunder arriving a few seconds later. The air began to smell of rain.

It took another fifteen minutes to get beyond the town, out the dirt road and close to Thomas Walker's ten-acre spread. There were only a few houses the past mile, nothing but desert ahead.

The first giant raindrop slapped my forehead like a wet cockroach, followed by a handful that thwacked the hood and windshield. The landscape rose gradually, then more abruptly, over a small ridge and then the bumpy road meandered for a quarter mile down into a dry wash. I muscled the Jeep as quickly as I could through a rutted gully at the bottom, then up the other side. The road was passable in a car, so long as it had good clearance. And so long as it was dry.

Cresting the bank on the other side, the dilapidated ranch house came into view a half-mile beyond. The rain picked up. The road was washboarded, making the Jeep, with its short wheel base, hop like popcorn if we moved too fast. We neared the house, a 1950s-looking wooden structure, tin roof, one lone green-trunked palo verde on the south side, slapping the eaves as the wind intensified.

The maroon Ford Econoline van sat in front of the house. I parked next to it and stepped out. A bolt of lightning struck the mesa, beyond the house but close now, thunder arriving just a second later. Rain fell steady in giant drops, soaking my t-shirt through. A palo verde branch screeched across the tin roof.

Solo followed me to the front door. I knocked. No answer. I knocked harder and waited. I pounded again and finally an old man in overalls, no shirt, opened the door, scowling. The wind blew back his white hair like a wispy cirrus cloud.

"Gonna break my door down," he said. "What the hell."

"Thomas Walker?"

"What?" We were only five feet apart but he squinted over his reading glasses to get a good look at me.

I spoke louder. "You Thomas Walker?"

"Who're you?"

"Eli Quinn," I said. "Looking for your son."

"Not here," the old man said. He pulled himself upright in an attempt to sound convincing.

I pushed the door open and walked past him. The living room was small and dark. An old color TV, perched on an end table, played a soap opera.

"Where's Clive?"

"What?"

"Clive," I shouted. "Where is he?"

"Don't know. He's a grown man, I don't keep track of him."

The last thing I wanted to do was rough up an 80-year-old man. I didn't have to. I heard the van start up.

Solo was first out the door. The van sped away. The rain was at full throttle now. The wind bent a palo verde branch to the ground. The dust was turning to mud. We sprinted to the Jeep.

Solo made the back seat in one leap. I jumped in and turned the key. A branch on the palo verde snapped and crashed to the ground as we pulled away. I huddled over the steering wheel, using the windshield to block the rain. It didn't work. I could barely see the van through the rain.

The van was heading out the way we came in, and getting smaller as it receded. I pushed the Jeep as hard as I could, the washboard road bucking the Wrangler. Our short wheelbase was a disadvantage, and the van pulled away.

We crested the rise ahead of the arroyo just as the van got stuck in the mud at the bottom. His door flung open. Clive Walker jumped out. He glanced our way, his long hair whipping around, then he scrambled up the other side. In less than half a minute we were at the bottom of the wash. Water had pooled around the van's tires and a small stream had developed at the deepest point, running under the van. The Jeep could handle the mud and a small stream, but the van blocked the only navigable path. Boulders upstream and a short but steep dropoff below. I backed up to higher ground in case the water rose, pocketed the keys, and we jumped out.

Clive might've escaped if he'd made it through the wash in the van. On foot, I knew we had him. He might have a gun, but I figured if he did, he'd have used it by now. That was a calculated risk we'd have to take. Solo didn't argue.

The muck was deep at the bottom of the arroyo. When Solo and I emerged above the bank on the other side, Clive was a good two-hundred yards out. He ran slowly, arms swinging inefficiently. He wouldn't last long. And I could run for miles, even in these conditions. So could Solo. We slogged through the muck for a minute and closed the gap. This is what Solo was trained for, so I gave him the command and he sprinted ahead.

I slowed to a jog, shoes soaked and heavy. If all went according to his training, Solo would get close, bark once. Clive Walker would know he was caught, would be terrified of the dog, and would stop running. Solo, using only as much force as necessary to subdue, would bare his teeth and growl until I got there. If Clive tried anything else, Solo would go to Plan B, which was never pretty.

Except none of that happened. A flash of lightning glinted off a blade, maybe four inches long. Clive Walker lunged with the knife and Solo fell to the ground.

CHAPTER 23

Dogs have incredible tolerance for pain, or maybe they just don't know how to express it. Either way, there was no way to know how bad Solo was. As I approached, he hauled himself up and balanced on three legs. He tried to come to me but stumbled into the mud and landed on his right side. I reached him, gently rolled him over. His right shoulder was caked in blood.

My throat swelled, tears filled my eyes. "No, Solo. Not now. Not here."

I took a deep breath to get my emotions under control, spread his fur and found the stab wound. Solo, eyes open, didn't blink, didn't shudder. He was stronger than I was. The rain began to wash the mud out. We waited. I looked down the road. The rain fell in sheets and the wind howled. Clive Walker was jogging away.

Solo's wound was clean, narrow and maybe an inch long, probably deep, still bleeding. I pulled my t-shirt off and pressed it against the wound. His breathing was rapid but even.

I could still catch Clive. If I waited too long, he'd be over the next rise and then, a few minutes later, could slip into a house, maybe steal a car, or disappear on foot. I watched him while pressing the wound with one hand, scratched Solo behind the ears with the other.

Nearly a minute later, Clive approached the rise. Decision time. I didn't want to leave Solo. But I couldn't let Clive get away.

"You OK, pal?"

He let his tongue slide out, gave me the winning Solo smile. I looked at Clive. Solo looked at him, too. Then he barked once. I nodded.

"I'll be right back," I said. "You stay here."

I held the t-shirt on the wound a moment longer, then I was up and running.

My trail-running shoes were soaked through but sturdy, laced up tight. Better than the boots Clive Walker wore. I struck a pace I'd used many times on six-mile runs. Fair bet there'd be a fight at the end of the run, so I didn't want to be winded when I caught him. That was the extent of my plan. I had to trust my training, my lethal hands and feet, to improvise.

The gap between us closed as Clive approached the rise. He crested just as I began the gradual climb. He started down the other side and slipped out of view. The rain was relentless. I had a quarter-mile to catch him before he'd reach the houses. I picked up the pace. At the top, I'd gained ground. No question I'd catch him—no more than fifty yards between us now. I slowed down to get my breathing under control.

Clive looked over his shoulder, saw me and stopped. He turned around to face me, knife in his left hand, right pulling his baseball cap down low. I slowed to a jog. Wind drove the rain sideways, felt like small rocks pelting my bare torso. Thunder was instant, deafening.

I walked the last twenty yards, fists at my sides, deep breaths.

We were ten feet apart. Clive's hat was pulled down, his

eyes deep and dark in there somewhere. I shouted. "Where's Joe Mack?"

"Fuck you." I could barely hear him above the storm.

"Jimmy Mendoza?"

Same answer. I took a step closer. A gust of wind pushed me forward a step and Clive back a step, blew his hat off, spilling hair across his face.

"Bo Rollins make you kill them?"

Clive laughed. A brief *ha*, loud and forced. "Bo Rollins…" He took a deep breath. "…isn't smart enough… for any of this."

"Who then?"

"You figure it out, wiseass."

And by then I had.

"Anyway, don't matter," he said. "No dog to protect you. You're a fuckin' dead man."

"Then let's get it over with," I said.

I moved in right away, knees bent, hands chest-high. Rule Number One in any fight to the death: Take whatever advantages you have. My breathing was under control. Clive was winded. I didn't want to give him any more time to recover.

But before we engaged fully, I also wanted to get a sense of Clive's fighting skills and style, without giving away what I was capable of. He was about six-three, just taller than me. He was strong. I knew he'd killed men in hand-to-hand combat. And he had a knife.

And so we danced a bit.

He lunged with the knife and I hopped back. Rule Number One in a knife fight: Stay away from the knife. Every other consideration is a distant second.

"Fuckin' punk," he said, wiping hair from his face.

I focused on the fight. No words needed. The sky hollered with thunder and spat more rain at us. He wiped the long hair out of his eyes. Vision was another advantage for me.

He began to circle to his right, the knife always belt-high and pointed my way. I feigned a boxer's roundhouse punch with my right hand and he lunged at it with the knife. I faked a wrestler's move on the other side, and he lunged at that.

This is what I'd hoped for: He was putting too much stock in his knife. I'd be using every tactic I knew, and now I had a good bead on his limited approach. The trick now was to get the knife away from him. The fight would be over if I could do that.

Sure, part of me wanted to kill Clive Walker now. But that wasn't my style. I thought of Solo. I'd subdue Clive, and yeah, he deserved a little bit more. Then I'd get some information out of him, and that would hurt a little. Him, not me. Maybe I could figure this whole case out.

I thought of Solo again. I needed to finish this now and get back to him.

I faked a low move and got Clive to lunge again, then as he drew the knife back I grabbed his right wrist with my left hand and pulled him down as my knee came up into his stomach. I reached over his head with my right arm and grabbed his left wrist to neutralize the knife, his head locked under my arm. All in less than a second. I gave him another knee to the stomach then pulled myself around his right shoulder and got both hands on his right forearm, pinning it and the knife to his body.

I'd underestimated Clive's strength. He heaved up and lifted me off the ground. I still had his arm and the knife pinned against him. When my feet touched the ground I jerked him backward and smashed my right elbow into his temple, but I slipped in the mud and the impact wasn't full. Clive swung up wildly with his free fist and caught my jaw, throwing me back. My phone and holster crunched on a rock, maybe saving me a badly bruised hip.

But I lost hold of him. I'd just botched the key move I had for disarming a knife-wielding man. I was on my back.

He was free. And I was out of tricks.

Clive rolled over onto his knees, dove at me. I aimed for his nose and kicked, connected with an eye instead. It wasn't enough to stop him but he'd be half blind for a moment. Yet he was atop me, his full weight pressing down. My left arm was trapped between us. He had my hair in his left hand. The rain punished my face and forced me to blink constantly. I'd lost my vision advantage. But I saw a shadow rise up—his left arm—and knew only that I couldn't let it come down.

With my right arm I reached not for the weapon but where his elbow should be. I caught it and pushed with everything I had to roll him over. We ended up face-to-face, grappling in the mud on our sides. He still had my hair, pulling. I still had his elbow, pushing. My left arm came free and I jabbed up with the shortest, most powerful punch I'd ever delivered, and heard his jaw crack. In the instant his left arm relaxed I shifted my grip to his wrist, shouted *Solo*, and pulled the knife down into Clive Walker's chest.

CHAPTER 24

The tall man lay on his back. Blinked, saw his own knife. Eyes failed.

Thunder, thunder, the thunder wouldn't stop. Chest on fire. Rain cool and comforting on his face. Arms and legs sinking into the earth, falling, no feeling.

Thoughts flitted by in an eternity that lasted a second. He'd failed. The one thing he was good at, and he failed. He hoped his father would be OK. His father had been tough, but always fair. Never hurt him, tried hard to raise him alone after his mother and sister died. He wished he'd done more for the old man. Lightning shattered the sky into a thousand pieces, seared his mind in a pain beyond anything. He tried to scream but nothing happened.

The rain stopped and the sun shined bright for an instant, then the darkest cloud he'd ever imagined rolled over him and came down, down, surrounding and choking, until the thinking stopped.

CHAPTER 25

You could say Clive Walker died at his own hand. You could say I killed him. Both would be true. Neither was what I'd hoped for. But I didn't enter the fight wanting to die, so I guess on some level I won. There'd be time later to worry about how that made me feel.

With the howling wind and driving rain, there was no point trying to feel for a delicate pulse. And there was no need. The knife had plunged into his heart. Blood was everywhere, spilling into the mud. If he wasn't dead yet, he would be soon, and there was nothing I could do about it.

And anyway, I was more worried about saving Solo.

I left the dying or dead Clive Walker in the mud, knife in his chest, and jogged back. Coming over the rise, I could see Solo where I'd left him, lying still. I sprinted. When I was just a few feet away he lifted his head and saw me. He made one slap in the muck with his tail. I got down on both knees and gave him an awkward hug, careful not to touch the wound. He licked my face and slapped his tail twice.

"You're gonna be OK boy," I said. "Got to get you back to the Jeep."

Solo didn't argue. I moved around to the other side of

him, squeezed my hands and arms underneath him. He whined but let me slowly pick him up. This German shepherd weighed 110 pounds. That's a lot to carry in a backpack. It's a whole lot to carry in front of you. But in a way, it was nothing. We trudged back down to the gully. The stream was as wide as the length of the van now, up to the bottom of the hubcaps. The rain let up. In the distance, the sky brightened underneath the back edge of the swift-moving thunderstorm. I considered waiting for the flash flood to subside. Solo whined. The water lapped the hubcaps. I knew it would rise further, even as the rain stopped, as miles of desert upstream funneled the past half-hour's rain into the arroyo.

Upstream, a wider, shallower spot offered less dangerous passage. I stepped into the brown, churning water with one foot. The water was halfway up my calf, the current tugging. I put my other foot in and we slogged through the growing flash flood, one careful step at a time.

The Jeep was well above the flood. I laid Solo on the back seat, got in, engaged the four-wheel drive and climbed out of the wash. On the bumpy drive back to Thomas Walker's house, the rain turned to sprinkles and the wind died down. Another hard shower gusted in and settled over the house just as we pulled up.

***

Thomas Walker opened his front door, rifle pointed at my chest, eyes squinting and glaring over the reading glasses. The door opened to a small kitchen with Formica counter tops. Behind him was a small dining room table with two chairs, and behind that a dark living room.

His eyes were untrusting slits. "The hell is going on?"

There were two options. The first one was sketchy. The old man had two hands on the gun, the left holding the stock just behind the trigger guard. It'd take him a split-second to get his finger on the trigger. Odds were better than even, maybe sixty-forty, I could knock the gun away in that split-second. I wasn't crazy about those odds. The other option was to disarm him with honesty.

"Mr. Walker, your son's a murderer," I said, speaking loudly so he could hear me.

"Says who," he said, waving the gun so it pointed at my face, then my crotch, then settling it chest-level.

"I'm a private investigator," I said. "Eli Quinn. I got a business card here."

"Show me."

I reached slowly and carefully into my jeans pocket with two fingers and pulled out a soggy, bent and frayed card, held it out. The old man snatched the card with his right hand, keeping the gun level by resting the stock on his thigh. I could have easily taken the gun in that instant, but we were making good progress, and he might prove useful if I could win him over.

He glanced at the card. "Hmph. Don't mean nothin'."

"What's Clive been up to lately?"

He glared at me. The gun barrel turned a circle. He pursed his lips. "Been around more than normal."

"Doing what?"

"Dunno. Out there a couple times." He pointed the gun out toward the driveway, swung it back at me. His eyes opened up, yellow, with a faraway look. "Then out back the other night. I don't see so well, but I could tell he had someone with him. Thinks I don't notice what's going on. He says it was some old friend, just showing him around." The old man blinked. He glanced at the gun, tilted it back up so it aimed squarely at my chest again. "What're you sayin'?"

"He killed a man," I said. "I'm certain of that. Maybe two. I'm hoping you can help me."

"Where's Clive?"

"He tried to kill me."

I let that sit there. The old man's eye twitched. He stared beyond me and his eyes glistened. The gun barrel inched downward.

He mumbled softly, defeated. "Dumb sumbitch."

"I'm sorry, Mr. Walker." There were a lot of things I could say, but I didn't see any advantage in saying them right now. So I said, "Dog's in the Jeep. He's hurt bad. Can I bring him inside?"

The old man lowered his head, gave a few short, tentative nods, and turned. He set the rifle on the kitchen table and walked back into the living room.

Solo whimpered just once when I scooped him out of the Jeep. I laid him on the floor of the kitchen. We were both soaked, mostly clean now from all the rain. I went back to the Jeep and fished the first aid kit out from the center console.

The wound was clean. The bleeding had stopped. I thought of trying to stitch it up but knew nothing about how. I wiped the wound with alcohol, put some antibiotic goo on it, placed a large sterile pad over it, made a few wraps with athletic tape, and then adhesive tape. It'd have to do for now.

The old man sat in his chair, staring at the TV, which was off. I walked over and stood in front of him. "Mr. Walker, can you tell me what Clive's been up to?"

He dropped his head, took his reading glasses off and talked into his lap. "Clive was never the smartest bulb in the room. He could do what he was told, but wasn't too good at figuring things out on his own. But he was a good kid, till his mama and sister died. After that, he started runnin' around, doing drugs. Come home beat up. Wouldn't listen to me. Boy needs his mama, you know?"

He looked up. I nodded. Then he turned his head away, talked to the wall.

"After high school, nobody would hire him, so he joined the Marines. I figured they might fix him. Made him worse.

He grew up some, sure, but the anger didn't go away, and Clive gots a short fuse."

I didn't correct his use of the present tense. I understood it. I'd done the same for a while after Jess died.

"Now he runs that half-ass bar, dug himself a mountain of debt. Wants me to sell this house, get some cash."

"What did you tell him?"

"This house, this land, it's all I got. Told him no way. Didn't see him for three months. Until this week."

"And what did you see this week?"

He looked back at me. He swallowed hard. "Clive's dead, ain't he?"

"I'm sorry, Mr. Walker. I had no choice."

The old man's yellow eyes got cloudier and wet. No tears came. "Bound to happen." He paused, bit his lip. "You keep pickin' fights, sooner or later you lose one."

"Tell me what Clive was doing this week," I said.

"Shed out front," he said. "Seen him come out of there a couple times. I don't see so good, but I seen that. Ain't been nothin' in that shed for years. He knows that. Maybe he's stashing stuff there. I dunno. Then I seen him walk out back with that man the other night. Didn't get a good look. But I think maybe the other man wasn't wantin' to go."

"Can you show me where?"

"Look out that window out back." He pointed. "You'll see a trail. Goes out a quarter mile or so, into a gulley. Clive used to play with those little green army men out there when he was a kid. He'd set up two teams, then throw rocks at them and blow 'em up with firecrackers. He loved that spot. Thick with mesquite trees. Thought nobody could see him down there."

"Is the shed locked?"

"Key's hanging in the kitchen, by the phone. Phone don't work though. They disconnected it last year."

I reached reflexively to my hip. The holster was there, my iPhone gone.

The key was hanging where he said. Solo swiveled his head to watch me go outside. The rain was light, the sky still gray, threatening yet more showers. But the thunder rumbled off to the south. I jogged to the shed and opened the lock, swung the door open.

Jimmy Mendoza lay on his side, mouth duct taped, hands and feet bound. His eyes were wide with fear until he realized it was me, and his whole body relaxed.

CHAPTER 26

"This is gonna hurt," I said, before ripping the duct tape off Jimmy's mouth.

"Ow. Goddamn, Quinn."

"Sorry. You OK?"

"Except for my face, my legs, my wrists." He held his hands out to me.

"I'll get something to cut the zip ties with," I said, and started to go.

"Wait!"

"What."

"Guy in a baseball cap…"

"He's no longer with us," I said.

Jimmy let his whole body relax, slumped back down to the plywood floor. I went to the Jeep and got a pair of wire snips from a tool box I kept in a lock box behind the rear seat, went back to the shed and cut Jimmy free.

He sat up, rubbed his wrists, felt the golf-ball-sized lump on the back of his head, one very much like mine.

"Quinn?"

"Yeah."

"Thank you. I don't know how the hell you found me.

But thank you. He was gonna…"

"I know," I said.

"What the hell is going on?"

"I'll explain in the Jeep. First tell me what happened to you."

"Not sure, really," he said. "I was leaving my office. I remember going out the door. Then I woke up here."

"You saw the guy?"

"I was coming to when he threw me in here. I barely got a look at him. He didn't say anything. Just ran his finger across his throat, shut the door and locked it. But I saw him, yeah. Tall guy, strong. Long hair."

"You don't know him?"

"Never seen him before," Jimmy said.

"Any reason you can think he'd come after you?"

Jimmy ran has hands through his short hair, laced them together behind his neck and looked up. "I talked to Bo."

"When?"

"Today."

"Where?"

"Met him out at Joe and Joanne's house. They asked me what was going on."

"And you didn't call me."

"We're not exactly BFFs."

"Fair enough," I said. "So Bo's back."

"Looked like they were getting ready to leave. She was packing."

"What'd you say to Bo?"

"I told them you suspected both of them," he said. "I asked them what the hell was going on. So they asked me what *I* thought."

"And you said?"

"I said I was starting to wonder the same thing. They denied it. Said you were making shit up, twisting the facts. Joanne can be pretty convincing. Bo, I'm not so sure. He was nervous, looked like he didn't know what to do."

"You were too close to them," I said. "They put a hit on you."

"I can't believe…"

"You talk to anyone else? Anything else I need to know?"

Jimmy rubbed his golf ball again, then asked: "How's Madison?"

"She was fine when I left an hour or so ago. Why?"

"I talked to her earlier today. We were both having the same feelings. I just hope she didn't do anything stupid. Not sure if you noticed, but she sometimes acts on impulse, doesn't think things through. Good kid, but…"

"We gotta go, Jimmy. Can you get in the Jeep on your own?"

"Sure."

"Hustle. I gotta get my dog."

***

With the van still blocking the way out, old man Walker gave me directions for another route back to Cave Creek. A little-used, pitiful excuse for a road that ran from behind the shed and across the mesa, onto a neighbor's land and back to Cave Creek.

A fence of rough wood posts and barbed wire separated the Walker property from the next.

"Cover your head," I shouted.

The Jeep plowed through the gate. Posts flew out of the way, wire screeched across the hood of the Wrangler and snapped. A post flew up, fell back and cracked the flat windshield, slid off to the side. The Jeep never slowed down.

The dirt road was better maintained on the neighbor's side, and I sped up. We still had to cross the arroyo. I drove down into it without slowing down. The water had dropped a few inches. We skipped across mud and plowed into the stream, parting it in two brown waves. We were out the other side, slipping and climbing, then onto the mesa and finally on pavement a moment later.

The Wrangler slid to a stop in front of the Buffalo Hide. I told Jimmy and Solo to stay in the Jeep, ran inside and found the bartender.

"Gimme your phone," I said. I must've been a sight, soaking wet, no shirt, blood on my hands.

He didn't hesitate.

I punched in Madison's number. She picked up on the second ring.

"Madison, it's Quinn. You OK?"

"Of course I'm OK. What's going on?"

"I found Jimmy. They were going to kill him. He's fine."

"What about my dad?"

I hesitated. I was ninety-nine percent sure Joe Mack was dead. I knew who did it. But I also knew who hired him to do it. No way to know how far they'd go.

"Quinn?"

I was just as sure Joe Mack's body would be partly decomposed by now, likely chewed at by coyotes, pecked at by buzzards. Probably washed down the gully he was dumped in. I didn't know if he'd be found at all. I didn't want to tell Madison any of that.

"Quinn?" She was shouting now. I had to say something, and it had to be honest, but most of it needed to be shared in person, not on the phone.

"We'll need to search the desert after the storm," I said.

She didn't say anything.

"Madison, listen. This isn't over. Jimmy saw Bo, out at your mom's house, and …"

She clicked off.

I shouted her name. Twice. *Goddamn that woman.* I dropped the phone and ran to the Jeep.

CHAPTER 27

It was a fifteen-minute drive from Cave Creek to the Mack's house in Pleasant. Made it in twelve. Madison's blue Tesla sat at a screwy angle in the driveway, a hasty park job. The garage door was wide open.

I told Solo to stay in the Jeep—he was breathing normally and the bleeding had stopped. If you didn't know how badly he was injured, you wouldn't guess. Jimmy and I ran through the garage, into the house, sprinted down the hall and into the living room.

Joanne Mack and Bo Rollins were sitting at opposite ends of the white couch. Their eyes went saucer wide at the sight of us. Madison stood behind the white club chair, legs shoulder width apart, pistol gripped with both hands. She pointed it briefly our way as we burst in, then trained it back on her mother, then Bo. We stopped ten feet away.

"Don't," I said.

"Give me one good reason why not."

"They didn't kill your father."

She glanced at me, a quick look, green eyes cold and fierce.

I took a step forward and stopped. "The man who killed

him is dead," I said.

"Who?"

"Give me the gun, I'll explain." I took a step forward, reached a hand out.

"But you said…" She kept the gun trained on her mother. "The divorce. And…"

"No more killing, Madison. You'll ruin your life."

"It's already ruined!" Her grief echoed in the cavernous living room.

"It seems like that now," I said. "But it's not."

"Madison," Jimmy said. "We can fix all this. I'll help you. Anything."

Her shoulders relaxed, just a degree. Her voice now lower. She eyed her mother, adjusted her grip on the pistol, waved it a bit. "They didn't do it?"

"They didn't kill anybody."

Madison shifted her weight. I spoke her name, softly, reached out again for the gun. Slowly she lowered it, held it in one hand at her side. Her eyes got a faraway look. I moved in and with a quick but gentle move took the gun from her, put the safety on, ejected the bullets and put them in my pocket, tucked the gun into my belt at the small of my back. Holding the gun reminded me of chasing down Jess' killer. The memories flooded back, Jess at the morgue when I had to ID her, one dark hole in her forehead, her killer's face just before I shot him, all of it. Images that used to fill my mind every day, images that would never leave, but that were faded now, sepia instead of color, torn around the edges. Then Sam took over my thoughts. We'd woken up together this morning for the first time. Unlike the last case, I'd handled this one more on my own. But I needed Sam now.

Madison was crying. I put my memories back in their mental box and put my arms around her.

Solo barked, just once. I hadn't heard him come in. Hobbling on three legs, he went past us, around the coffee table, got in front of Bo to block any exit he might try to make from the couch, and barked three more times. That was three more than normal. Then he just snarled.

"Let me see your arm, Bo."

"Fuck you."

"Dog can finish what he started. I just say so."

"OK, OK." Bo put his hands up, ever the tough guy with, in the end, no spine. Solo did that to people. He rolled his left sleeve up, revealing a forearm wrapped from the elbow to wrist.

Solo barked one more time, looked over at me to make sure I heard him.

Joanne bolted from the couch, toward the front door. Jimmy Mendoza could've simply stood in her way, maybe grabbed her arm. She wouldn't have had any chance of getting past him. Instead he wound up and clocked her square in the face. Joanne tumbled into the coffee table and shattered it. Glass flew everywhere and she hit the floor with a thud. Jimmy grabbed his hand, which was almost surely broken.

Madison's whole body jerked. I held her tighter.

Blood spilled from Joanne's nose. She blinked, looked over at her daughter, opened her mouth as if to speak, then closed her eyes, laid back and covered her face with both hands.

Solo had stopped snarling. Bo hadn't moved. Joanne's shoulders shook—maybe, possibly, a sign of grief, but who knew.

Madison had stopped crying. She lifted her head and searched my face. She looked scared, vulnerable, for the first time. A thin trickle of makeup ran down one cheek. She pushed back, wiped tears with both hands, spoke in a level tone. "You said they didn't do it." She didn't sound angry. Just confused.

"I said they didn't kill anybody."

"Who killed my father?"

"Bo and your mother hired a guy, ex-Marine who owed Bo a lot of back rent. Leverage. Probably offered to wipe the debt and maybe kick in some more cash."

"You lied to me," she said.

"Technically, I didn't," I said. "But yeah, we're even. And you're not going to jail."

Madison stared at me without glaring. She looked at her mother.

"I'm sorry," I said. What I meant was I understand what it's like to lose the most important person in your life, and right now it feels like your life is over. But I promise, it's not. You'll find a way forward, eventually you'll have closure, and you'll be happy again. The weight of sadness will always be with you, but happiness isn't something that exists in a vacuum. It's the flip side of sadness, and you need one to know the other. Instead, I just said "I'm sorry" again.

Madison Mack's face collapsed. Every feature seemed to sink or sag. I knew what she was feeling. Hollowness, nothingness. She would not want to talk or listen right now. She pursed her lips and nodded, understanding, then closed her eyes, let her head sink forward and shook it slowly, either in recognition or disbelief or both.

CHAPTER 28

S am Marcos was curled against me, head on my chest, arm over and around me. She was naked. I wanted to be.

"Hey sleepy," she said.

"What time is it?"

"Ten-thirty."

"Impossible. I never sleep this late."

"You had a rough day."

Sam had met me at the sheriff sub-station, where I was stuck past midnight explaining everything that had happened, or at least what I knew of it. We'd left the Jeep there and she drove me home, got me showered. I don't even remember crawling into bed.

"You been here all this time?"

"Nope. Been up since six. I ate, went to the paper to help them with this story."

"You're not writing it?"

"Zee says I need to lay off writing about your exploits, now that we're a thing."

Nick Zee, managing editor of *The Arizona Republic*. Great guy. "Smart decision."

"Then I met Beach for a quick coffee at Lulu's. He says hi and congratulations."

"But you're not wearing anything," I said.

"Not now. I was earlier. I have a plan now that doesn't call for much attire."

"Good plan," I said.

The haze in my head cleared and the warm and comfortable feelings of Sam gave way to thoughts of Clive Walker's face as I'd rolled him onto his back and left him on the ground, knife stuck in his chest. Madison Mack's sadness. Her mother's busted face. Jimmy Mendoza smacking her. Bo Rollins' utter ineptitude. All the nudity, greed, death.

"Where's Solo?" I asked.

"Still at the vet. I called and they said he'll be fine but it'll take a while. The cut was deep but clean. Hopping out of the Jeep at the Mack's house wasn't the smartest thing to do."

"Solo picks right over smart sometimes."

"Like someone else I know," Sam said. "Anyway, you can pick him up this afternoon. He'll need to be really lazy for a while."

"Solo's good at being lazy," I said.

"Solo's good at a lot of things."

I smiled at that. "What else?"

"They found Joe Mack's body. About a quarter-mile down from where you said."

I sighed. "Madison know?"

"Beach told her."

"He's good at things like that."

"He is."

We lay still for a moment. I squeezed Sam's shoulder. She nuzzled into me.

"I've never killed anyone before," I said.

"You almost did once before," she said. "On Murder Mountain."

"But I was able to stop myself."

"You did what you had to do this time. It was the right thing."

"Doesn't make it feel good."

"But it feels better than if you killed someone for no good reason."

I nodded.

"It might happen again, Quinn. This is what you do now."

I nodded.

"And you're really good at it."

"I didn't want to kill him," I said. "But I'm glad it wasn't the other way around. I can't imagine not being here with you. I can't imagine us not being us."

I expected Sam to say something. Instead she twirled a finger on my chest.

"Quinn?" She sounded timid. It was something Sam never sounded.

I waited.

"The *Times* called."

I closed my eyes, felt my stomach surge into my throat. She waited for me.

"Which *Times*?"

"You know which one," she said.

Life is funny. When things are tough, it slogs along in slow motion, a movie with no apparent end. Sadness, strife and stress are life's favorite bedfellows. Let a little sunshine in, and suddenly life speeds up, a raucous comedy in fast motion that you know won't last long.

"They want you working remote or in the office?"

Sam breathed in deeply, breathed out long. Of course I knew.

"Nobody better than you," I said. "It was only a matter of time."

"I don't have to go," she said.

I opened my eyes. She looked up at me. Her finger

stopped twirling. I wanted to agree with her. I wanted to come up with a million reasons why she should turn them down.

"You can't not go," I said. "It's what you've aimed for your whole career. It's what you're best at. It's what you do. And you do important things, *good things*. They need you. The world needs you."

Sam Marcos stared at me with the most amazing brown eyes anyone has ever seen, sad and happy and confused and in love all at once. I took a mental snapshot to hold onto forever.

"We should make love first," I said.

"You mean now."

"And later."

"Good plan."

ABOUT THE AUTHOR

Robert Roy Britt is the author of *First Kill*, *Closure* and *Drone*, the first three books in the Eli Quinn detective series, and the short prequel *Murder Mountain*. His first thriller, *5 Days to Landfall*, publishes Nov. 14, 2016. He lives in Arizona with his wife, their youngest son and two dogs. You can visit his website at robertroybritt.com.

ACKNOWLEDGEMENTS

Writing can be a lonely occupation. But at many stages in the creation and completion of a story, the help and encouragement of others is vital. I'm grateful for the insights and suggestions big and small from my fellow authors at the Internet Writing Workshop: Silvia, Dave, Virginia, Mark P., Mark K., Jennifer, Elaine, Bob, Mairhi, Carmel, Michele, Bill, Francene, Elma, Carolyn, Lee, Brent and others. A huge thanks to my sharp-eyed editor, Lauren Craft, who waded through more than normal on this one and was instrumental in providing direction and polish. And to the most helpful reader of early drafts, S.L.B., I hope the finished story lives up to expectations.